Deadly Offerings

Alexa Grace

Deadly Offerings

This book is a work of fiction. Names, characters, places and incidents are products of the author's imagination or are used fictitiously. Any resemblance to actual events or locales or persons, living or dead, is entirely coincidental.

Cover design by Christy Carlyle at Gilded Heart Design.
Edited by Vicki Braun and Melissa Anne McGee.
Revised December 2014 by Melissa Anne McGee.

ISBN-13: 978-1-4700-3655-3
ISBN-10: 147003655X

Published in the United States of America.

For Melissa and Megan

Acknowledgments

I want to express my appreciation to my family and friends. Without their love, encouragement and support, this book would not have been possible.

I offer a sincere thank you to my friend and editor, Vicki Braun, who painstakingly edited this book.

I also extend my gratitude to my daughter and editor, Melissa Anne McGee, who edited the revised version of this book in January 2015.

Much appreciation goes to the Beta Reader Team who devoted their personal time to review each page for the revision of this book: Gail Goodenough, Barrie MacLaughlin, and Debra Snyder.

Chapter 1

The man leaned against an oak tree, smoking a cigarette, watching as a flood of college students made their exit from the Liberal Arts building. He scanned the crowd until he spotted her struggling with her backpack. He'd hacked her email and printed the class schedule she'd been kind enough to share with her email buddies. Stupid bitch. Rachel Mitchell was almost too easy to stalk.

He watched her stop and talk to a tall, dark haired boy. She wore a black t-shirt with the letters P-I-N-K spread across her chest, and the boy was having a hard time keeping his eyes off her breasts. He'd watched her put the shirt on earlier from outside her open bedroom window in her ground-floor apartment.

He kept an eye on her as she made her way across the parking lot to her car. There was a two-hour break between classes, and she usually went to her apartment during that time. He headed toward his Mustang. This may be the day her life gets changed forever, and not in a good way. This may be the day he'd been patiently waiting for—a day with no witnesses, no struggle, and a ride in the trunk of his car. Payback time, and it was long overdue for Rachel Mitchell.

And very, very soon, Anne Mason-Long would find out that payback is hell in a very personal, very painful way.

The Front Page Bar used to be Michael Brant's favorite hangout, but too many beers and twenty-one-year-old busty cheerleader types had lost their appeal. It had been at least two years since he'd visited. He wouldn't be here tonight if it weren't for Edward

Casey insisting he needed to talk to him, and it had to be here away from the office. Undoubtedly, Edward would do his best to butter him up to get consideration for the deputy prosecutor position he had open. He spotted Edward at the bar and headed for him.

The bar seemed filled to capacity as Anne Mason-Long waded through the crowd toward her friends' table. Cheri and Jan, both waving wildly at her, had been her friends since college. She reached them and slid into the booth, nearly knocking over their huge margaritas. The waitress arrived with a margarita for Anne, along with a large basket of nachos and a spicy, cheesy dip.

"How is our soon-to-be-free girl doing?" Cheri asked as she scanned Anne's expression. It had been more than sixty days since Anne had filed for the divorce. Cheri thought she should have gotten a couple of years ago. One of the things she loved about Anne was her loyalty. However, there was a limit to how long a woman should be loyal to a cheating, gambling, lying asshole. In Cheri's opinion, 2.5 seconds was enough time to give the jerk before she threw his stuff out the front door.

"I'm good. I've been so busy at work; there hasn't been much time to think about the divorce," Anne said.

"When is D-Day?" Jan looked her over. Anne looked tired, but other than that, she was as beautiful as ever, with shoulder-length auburn hair, dressed in a red silk tee and snug, faded jeans. The sooner Anne's divorce hearing was over the better. She needed time to heal, and then get on with her life.

Anne sighed. "Allan is contesting the property settlement, so there's a hearing tomorrow."

"You can't be serious! That takes nerve, after all the money he's lost in the casinos. What does he want?" Cheri exclaimed.

"What doesn't he want?"

Jan perked up in her seat and whispered to Anne, "Don't look now, but there's a gorgeous hunk sitting at the bar, checking you out big-time."

Anne laughed. "Very funny, Jan. The last time I got checked out was at the grocery store."

"That's not true, and I'm serious," Jan insisted. "Pretend

you're looking for someone in the crowd, and check out the tall guy in the black leather jacket at the bar."

Anne sipped her drink, then nonchalantly scanned the room, starting at the door and ending at the bar. "I think he's looking at you not me."

"Seriously? Have you had your eyes checked lately? His eyes are super-glued on you," said Jan.

Cheri purred, "He looks like one of those hot male models from an Armani ad."

"Would you two please stop staring?" Anne rolled her eyes and sipped her margarita.

She glanced over at the bar. The hunk in question was sitting next to a man wearing a suit, but was clearly not listening to a word he said. He did seem to be looking at her. Once their eyes met, he shot her a devastating smile that made her catch her breath. A blush burned her cheeks as she looked away.

"See, I told you he was checking you out," Jan said with a smirk.

Michael sipped his beer and continued to stare at one of the most attractive women he had seen in a long, long time. Edward Casey ignored him and droned on about his prosecutor qualifications. "Hey, Edward," he interrupted.

"Yeah."

"Do you come to this bar very often?"

"Sure. Most attorneys do, because it's so close to the courthouse. Why?"

"See that group of three women in a booth over there? Do you know the one with long red hair?"

"No." Edward shook his head. "I've seen the blonde she's with, but I've never seen the redhead here."

Michael just nodded, and Edward returned to his self-sale pitch.

"Jan, can we talk about something else? This conversation is pretty inappropriate, since I'm not even divorced yet," said Anne.

"Anne, for once, would you please give yourself a break? Maybe the thing you need right now is a fling," said Jan. Cheri nodded her head in agreement.

"I'm not a fling kind of girl."

"Yeah, like we missed that one in college. It was all we could do to get your nose out of your books long enough to come up for air." Jan poked Cheri in the ribs and they both laughed.

"I wasn't that boring, was I?"

"No, honey, you weren't boring. You just didn't have much fun," said Jan.

"You two had enough fun for all of us."

"So when was the last time you had sex?" Jan demanded, smiling at how quickly Anne blushed.

"You did not just ask me that."

"Has it been months? Or years?"

"It's nobody's business." It had been two years, not that Anne would ever admit it. She could probably be a nominee for a book of records—married woman who had gone the longest without sex.

"Just saying. Time might be right for a fling."

"No thanks," said Anne. She took a quick look at her watch. It was nearly eight o'clock.

"Why are you looking at your watch? You're not leaving yet. You just got here."

"I've got a big dog at home with a huge appetite, and he usually eats his dinner at six. I really need to get home before he starts eating the furniture."

"Anne, we didn't mean to make you uncomfortable. Don't go."

"I love you two. You didn't make me uncomfortable, but I really do need to go." Anne threw her purse over her shoulder, then hugged each of them, promising to get back together soon. She headed for the door weaving in and out of people as she went.

Outside, Anne walked toward her SUV, not noticing the heavy drunk man who was following her, until he grabbed her shoulder and yanked her around to face him.

"Hey, Red. You're not leaving, are you?" He slurred his words and smelled of stale beer and body odor.

Wordlessly she backed away a step, rummaging in her purse for her pepper spray, but couldn't find it. Damn. Her eyes scanned the parking lot, looking for someone to call for help; it was filled with cars, but no people.

"Babe, you just can't leave until we do some dancin'." The man grabbed Anne, forcing her against his body as he simulated a slow dance.

She pushed at his chest and snapped, "Back off."

"Not a chance, Red." Still dancing, he had her body in a vise grip that threatened to cut off her air, as he moved her toward a parked Hummer. He hard-pressed Anne against the vehicle so she couldn't move.

Anne desperately wanted to kick him in the groin, but she couldn't free her legs. She turned her face away as he bent down to kiss her.

"Let her go, and I mean now." A low, growl sounded behind them, and the man loosened his hold.

"Fuck you, and mind your own business," the drunk shot back. The words were barely out of his mouth when a huge man in a leather jacket slammed into the drunk, knocking him to the pavement.

Rubbing his face, the drunk glanced back to see a tall, muscular man standing over him, fists clenched, ready for a fight that he couldn't possibly win—drunk or not. He scrambled to his feet, and headed back to the bar. The man in the leather jacket turned to Anne, who was staring at him in amazement.

"Are you okay?" He moved toward her and brushed the hair out of her face.

"Yes, thank you." She looked up at him and immediately recognized the man at the bar. He was even better-looking up close, brown eyes with glints of golden lights, and a ruggedly handsome face.

"I'll walk you to your car," he offered.

"No, thanks. I just found my pepper spray. I can take care of myself," Anne said as she lifted the small can from her purse. She glanced back as she walked away. He was leaning against the Hummer watching her, and she felt a surge of lust shoot through her body like a bullet. Anne sighed when she reached her car, and thought of the cold shower she'd have when she got home.

There was one parking space left in the courthouse parking lot, and attorney Michael Brandt had just passed it. He threw his silver metallic Escalade EXT in reverse, but it was too late, a car was moving in his direction. He cursed, put the gear in drive, and headed around the lot again. He eased in the lane where he saw the empty space, just in time to see a blue Honda CRV move into it. Damn. This incident was just one more thing to add to what was turning out to be a crap day.

Earlier, he'd broken his coffee pot; which meant no caffeine in his caffeine-starved body. That did nothing to help his bad mood and burgeoning headache. If that weren't enough, he got pulled over for speeding and got a ticket from a cop he used to work with. The traffic stop made him late for court, and now there was no place to park. Michael's client was probably looking all over the courthouse for him; not that he cared. The more he met with Allan Long, the more he disliked him, and representing the jerk in his contested divorce proceeding was not going to be the highlight of his legal career.

Anne Mason-Long grabbed her briefcase out of the back seat of her SUV. She swung her cross-body leather purse over her head and ran up the courthouse steps, once she reached them. If there was one appointment she didn't want to be late for, it was her divorce hearing. The sooner this train wreck was over, the better. By the time she passed through security, her head was pounding like a drum. What was she thinking when she passed the Starbucks drive-through without getting her daily Grande Mocha Latte? She needed a caffeine fix and she needed it *now.*

Once through security, she stopped a man with a court employee badge and asked him where she could get some coffee. He looked her over from head-to-toe, then focused on her breasts as he gave her directions down the hall. She thanked him and as she walked away, she wished she had the nerve to ask, "Don't you wish breasts could talk?"

She rushed down the hall and pushed on the "Court Employees Only" door and was relieved to find the room empty. The last thing she needed was to be boycotted from the break room, more importantly the coffee pot, because she wasn't an employee.

When Anne reached the coffee pot at the end of the room, she realized it was empty. There should be a law against people who drain the last drops of coffee and don't make more. Who does that? She pulled open cabinet doors until she found coffee, which she dumped in the coffee maker, then pushed the button for the hot water. She eyeballed her watch and realized she had five minutes before her hearing started.

The door flew open and an attractive, harried man raced in. He threw his briefcase on a table and sprinted toward her. She backed up a few feet, then realized he was heading toward the coffee pot—not her.

"It should be ready in a few minutes," she said as she looked him over. He was a man her girlfriends would describe as eye candy, with broad shoulders and the hard-sculpted body of a professional athlete. At this moment, she didn't care how hot he was; if he touched the coffee before she got a cup, he was going down.

He ignored her and retrieved a couple of Styrofoam cups from a cabinet above the sink. Apparently, he knew his way around the break room. He picked up the pot and put one of the cups under the hot stream of coffee. Once it was filled, he handed it to her, and then filled the other cup.

She thanked him and rushed to the condiment area to add cream and sugar. She sipped the brew, discovered it was too hot, and flowed like molten lava down her throat. She hurried to the door but he beat her to it, threw it wide open, then waited for her to go through.

She found Courtroom #3 and was surprised to find that her handsome coffee comrade entered the room just behind her. When she reached a long table on the right side of the room, she pulled out a chair, placed her briefcase underneath and sat down to have some one-on-one time with her coffee.

He watched her as he moved toward a long table on the left side of the room. He sat down and really looked at her for the first time. She was beautiful. Evidently, when he was in need of a caffeine fix, he not only got a headache but became blind as well.

Her long hair was auburn with streaks of gold, tied back in a high ponytail, her lips full and sexy. Her skin was pale, and the contrast made her eyes an even darker blue. She was shapely, and her long legs went on forever. She must be a *new* attorney in town, otherwise he had no clue how he'd missed seeing her before. She did look vaguely familiar, but she had a face and body a man did not forget easily—especially this man.

He moved to her table and tapped her shoulder. "Excuse me; I don't believe we've met." When she stood up, he extended his hand to her. "My name is Michael Brandt."

She shook his hand, smiled and answered, "Nice to meet you, and thanks for the coffee." She looked into his eyes and noticed they were brown with glints of gold. He had the kind of grin that was irresistibly devastating. Recognition kicked in and she realized she was gazing into the face of the man at the bar who rescued her the night before.

"You're…" she began.

Before she could continue, an elderly man moved in beside her, pulling on her arm to talk to him as he sat down.

Michael moved back to his table, pulled open his briefcase, and then scanned the courtroom looking for his client. Where was he anyway? In fact, where was the soon to be ex-wife? He turned his gaze back to the gorgeous attorney at the next table. It was odd, but she looked familiar, though he couldn't place her. He didn't get her name, not that it mattered, because he fully intended to ask her out for some decent coffee as soon as the hearing ended.

Just as the judge entered the room, Michael's client slid into his chair beside him as if it were third base.

"Nice of you to join us," Michael said, not bothering to hide the sarcasm in his tone. "Since you're here, do you have any idea where your soon-to-be ex-wife might be?"

Allan Long settled in his chair, then looked to the table to the right of them and said, "Yeah, she's sitting right over there next to her attorney, Stanley Delaney.

Michael groaned. How could he have made a mistake like that? She wasn't an attorney; she was the opposing client. Just when he thought his day couldn't get worse, he noticed Anne Mason-Long glaring at him. No doubt she realized that earlier she had been sharing coffee and pleasantries with her husband's attorney.

Movement at the far end of the room distracted Anne. Several people had entered the courtroom and were finding seats in the gallery seating. Her face heated with the humiliation that strangers would hear this private, low moment of her life. She told herself to focus on blocking out their presence. Wasn't blocking out the unpleasant her specialty in her marriage to Allan?

She felt a tension ride her body. She wished this ordeal was over.

Stanley Delaney watched her as he organized some papers in front of him. His long fingers pushed back his eyeglasses which were sliding down his nose. Her appearance worried him. She'd lost weight and her face was pale; dark smudges marked the area beneath her eyes. But what did he expect? For the past two years she'd experienced one loss after the other.

"Anne, would you like for me to get you anything?"

She studied his face for a second then said, "Stanley, I don't need or want your pity. If you're sitting over there feeling sorry for me, you're wasting your time. I'm a big girl. I'm not the freckled-faced kid who used to sit on your knee."

Stanley's face registered surprise, then his mouth formed a grin. The girl had spunk. She had been through so much the past two years: losing her baby and her beloved grandmother, then losing a woman who was more of a mother than her own had ever been, while watching her marriage dissolve in bitter pieces around her.

Anne watched him return to his papers and sipped coffee that was now cold and bitter. This was one of those times she wished she could go back to being the little girl who played in Uncle Stanley's office. That seemed like a lifetime ago. She looked around the room, avoiding the area of space that Allan and his attorney occupied.

A bailiff announced there would be a twenty-minute delay for the hearing.

Anne watched as three elderly spectators left the room through the thick wooden doors of the rear exit. She surmised they were heading for the snack machine at the end of the hall for a cold drink. She hoped they were observing the court proceedings as an escape from the stifling hot and humid Indiana late summer weather, rather than a perverse form of entertainment. The air conditioner rattled feebly as it warded off the stagnant air outside.

She thought of a promise she'd made long ago. She closed her eyes and formed an image of Marion. Thank God, she was not here to witness this.

It was the coldest day of winter, but the chill outside was nothing compared to the cold dread she felt as she entered Marion's hospital room. Quick tears had come to her eyes as she looked down at Allan's mother. What was once a vibrant, powerful woman now seemed a lifeless shell of a human. The cancer that had ravaged her body had taken everything but her mind. Anne swallowed hard and pulled Marion's hand into her own.

"Hello, dear one." She whispered.

Anne willed herself not to cry. Marion would hate that.

"Anne, my love. Thank you for coming."

"You couldn't have kept me away."

"I haven't much time…" Marion began.

"Please don't say that."

Marion smiled weakly and went on. "You're like a daughter to me. Your coming into my family was my son's greatest gift to me."

"Please, I…"

"Don't interrupt. What I am about to say is very important to me. I'm about to ask you to make a promise to a dying woman…a promise I have no right to ask."

"You must know that you can ask me to do anything. I love you."

"Once I'm gone, you'll be contacted by my attorney about my will."

"I don't want to talk about your will, Marion."

"Stop interrupting me." She said sharply, her eyes deepening. "I've stipulated in the will that you are to inherit the Golden Acres Farm. You're the only one who loves that land as much as I do; the only one who has the guts and gumption to run it like it should be run."

"I can't let you do this. Allan should have the farm, not me."

"Allan? Seriously? I may be old, but I'm not blind and stupid. Allan is my son, my only child, and I love him. But I know his flaws. He drinks too much. He stays out too late doing God knows what. He gambles to excess. I've had to bail him out way too many times." She paused, tightening her fragile grip on Anne's hand.

"You know about that?"

"Yes, my dear, I know about that and more. I know about the other women. You've made a valiant effort to shield me from my son's vices. But there's no need for that. If my Harry had done half the things Allan has done to you, I'd have divorced his ass long ago. Thank God, Harry was a saint. Our son is *no* saint. Just glad Harry didn't live to see the man that Allan has become."

A nurse came in with a breakfast tray and Marion dismissed her with a wave of her hand. She turned her attention back to Anne. "I know you're considering divorce."

Anne's eyes widened with surprise. "Well, I…"

"There's no need to explain." Marion paused briefly to examine Anne's reaction and braced herself for what she was about to say. "Allan is visiting me this afternoon and I'll tell him about my will. Allan will receive a generous monthly check from the trust I set up for him. I intend to tell him that the Golden Acres Farm will be your property and yours alone."

"Marion, you cannot do this."

"I damn well can and did."

"Allan will fight me in court for the farm. You know he will."

"If he does, he loses that generous monthly check from his trust fund. I've stipulated that in the will."

"Marion, I cannot accept…"

"You can and you will. Promise me, Anne. Please promise me. Give an old dying woman some peace. You must promise me that you will care for my farm."

Anne was jolted back to the present by the bailiff announcing the return of Judge Warriner.

"If there is no objection, I'd like to move this hearing into my chambers," said Judge Warriner.

A wave of relief washed over Anne as Stanley began packing his briefcase with files from the table. She would get the privacy she needed.

She glanced at Michael Brandt. The room was large but when Michael stood, he seemed to fill it. He was huge; at least 6'5" with the broad shoulders and the hard, toned muscles of an athlete, she'd noticed in the break room. His size alone was intimidating. He certainly didn't look like the attorneys Anne knew, pale and thin. Her initial instinct warned that he was a man who could be ruthless—with or without his caffeine.

Today he wore an expensive navy suit tailored to fit his big frame. He was one of the most handsome men she had ever seen. And wasn't it just her luck that he was Allan's attorney? And wasn't it inappropriate that she was ogling Allan's attorney at her divorce hearing?

Once inside the judge's chambers, they sat at a conference table facing each other. The judge sat at the end of the table. Stanley and Anne sat on one side, Allan and Michael on the other. The judge turned around and poured some coffee into his cup from the pot on the table behind him.

Michael told himself he should stop looking at Anne Mason-Long. But he couldn't stop looking at her. What was it that was so familiar about her? Shit. She was the woman from the bar last night. She looked different with her hair pulled back and dressed in a suit. Can this situation get any more complicated?

The judge started the proceeding, "According to my notes, Anne and Allan have met several times to discuss the 50/50 division of their assets but have not come to agreement as to the Property Settlement Agreement. This hearing is scheduled to review any additional information regarding the property division you'd like me to consider before I reach a judgment. Mr. Delaney, do you have new information to share?"

Stanley pulled a file from his briefcase and slid it across the table to the judge.

"In this file, you will find Allan Long's financial records from his bank. In addition, I am including records of gambling losses of $750,000 from the French Lick Casino here in Indiana as well as the Venetian, Casino Royale and Mandalay Bay Casinos in Las Vegas. Mr. Long has also exceeded his credit limit on both his Visa and MasterCard and owes both a total of $50,000.

I submit these records as evidence of the deliberate wasting of marital assets through Mr. Long's long-term gambling."

Michael glared at Allan. His client shared nothing of his gambling and credit card debt prior to the hearing. Allan had claimed that his wife's spending was driving him into the ground. He realized Allan was not only the asshole he thought he was, but a liar, too. He cursed himself for taking his case.

"Where did you get that information?" Allan was incredulous. "You bitch," he shouted at Anne across the table.

"One more outburst like that and I will find you in contempt. Do you understand me, Mr. Long?"

"Yes, sir."

"Mr. Brandt, please advise your client not to speak until Mr. Delaney has finished," chastised Judge Warriner.

Michael Brandt's eyes darkened as he whispered something in Allan's ear. Allan pushed back in his chair, his expression in a pout like that of a small child who didn't get his way.

"Mr. Delaney, do you have additional information to share?"

"Not at this time."

"I see," said the judge as he scribbled some notes on a legal pad.

"Mr. Brandt, do you have additional or new information to share?"

"What Mr. Delaney did not say is that Mr. Long's family invested $50,000 in his wife's computer company, Computer Solutions, Inc. Mrs. Long is a partner in this company. Her partnership is valued at $500,000. And, as you know, Mr. and Mrs. Long own a home that is valued at $300,000. In addition, Mrs. Long was given a farm last year that has been in Allan's family for over 100 years and is valued at one million dollars. should be considered in the 50/50 division of property."

Anne cringed. The reason he was sharing this information

was crystal clear. Allan wanted money and a lot of it. More than that, he wanted the farm so he could sell it, so he would have more money to gamble. Allan was incensed that his mother left her the farm.

When she'd asked Allan for a divorce, he seethed with anger. "Sure you can have your divorce, but it will cost you big-time. It will cost so much that you may have to sell your precious Golden Acres Farm—which should be mine in the first place!"

Stanley Delaney nearly jumped out of his chair. "Judge, the farm that Mr. Brandt refers to was an inheritance from Allan's mother, Marion, to Anne. She specifically named Anne to inherit the farm. Allan inherited a trust fund with monthly payments of five thousand dollars."

"The farm will *not* be considered during this property division. If Mr. Long wants to contest his mother's will, he can do that in another hearing," said Judge Warriner.

Anne nudged her attorney, "I want to talk with you privately."

"Your honor, could we have a ten-minute break so that I can talk with my client."

"Granted."

The judge headed for his office as Michael and Allan left the room.

"Allan can have the money he wants. Offer him $650,000," said Anne. A frozen, bitter mask covered her face.

"What? You can't mean that. You don't have that kind of money."

"I'll sell the house we shared, and I'll sell my partnership in the company. It's time I moved to the farm anyway. I can't run Golden Acres as it deserves part-time. I promised Marion I'd take care of the farm, and I will."

"Anne, as your attorney, I must advise you that you are not acting in your own best interests. As your attorney, I must advise you…"

"Draw up the papers, Stanley. It's only money. I want my life back. Your job is to get me this divorce and get me out of this nightmare. Period."

She didn't see Michael Brandt near the floor-to-ceiling window in the hallway when she left the courtroom. But he saw her. He was waiting for her. He scanned her face as she passed him, her dark blue eyes angry and focused ahead of her. She had seemed upset and he wanted to make sure she was okay. He couldn't believe she caved and gave Allan that much money. If he were in her place, he certainly wouldn't have. The guy was a loser. That money would flow through his fingers like water.

He thought he might be losing it. Since when did he care about whether an opposing client was okay? Since when did he give a damn about the impact he had on them? What kind of an attorney was he anyway? Hadn't his mentor always told him, "It isn't personal. Nothing about the law is personal." Well, if it wasn't personal, why did he feel like such a freaking bully?

He never should have taken this case. He had misgivings about Allan that started with their first meeting. He should have bailed then. He should have told Allan that he wouldn't represent him. He should have followed his gut.

He was glad he was leaving his law practice. Damned glad. He was just too good at his job, and too many jerks like Allan were winning cases they had no business winning. He'd attained freedom for too many people who were guilty and were now walking the streets, probably repeating past mistakes. He couldn't do it anymore. He needed a fresh start.

Michael watched Anne as she left the courthouse, her shoulders straight, and her long legs taking purposeful strides toward a Blue Honda CRV. Something heated inside him. There was something about her, or maybe it was his year-long hiatus from sex.

And for reasons he didn't understand, he wanted to see her again. And at the same time, he realized his chances of that were between slim to none.

Anne peered into her refrigerator. Not a piece of junk food in sight. She opened the freezer. How could she be out of ice cream at a time like this?

She had to get out of the house. Tonight bad memories hung

over her like a thundercloud. She relived the humiliating divorce hearing over and over, becoming angrier each time.

She tried to sleep. No success. She got out of bed and pulled on a pair of jean shorts, a black glittery Lady Gaga tank top, and her Reeboks. She'd go for a drive to clear her head. It was close to midnight, but with any luck, she'd find someplace open to stock up on junk food.

She backed her SUV out of the garage, shoved the gear to drive and moved down the street, windows down, the breeze whipping her ponytail about her face. She drove down Route 40 until she reached a section of fast food restaurants, bars and a mini-mart. The mini-mart didn't look busy so she parked in front.

She grabbed a shopping basket and strode down an aisle of the store picking up Reese's Peanut Butter Cups, Butterfinger candy bars, tortilla chips, a jar of salsa, and a quart of soda as she went. She moved to the refrigerator case and eyed the selection of ice cream. She pulled out a couple of cartons of Ben & Jerry's Red Velvet Cake, then headed to the teenaged cashier, whose eyes were plastered on her long legs.

She paid for the items, whirled around and slammed into the hard chest of a tall man entering the store. Her items tumbled from the bag. The salsa jar rolled across the store as did the bottle of soda. The man uttered "sorry" as he bent to help her pick up the items. He picked up the salsa and put it in her bag. He moved down the aisle to get the soda that had rolled under a freezer then turned toward her. In a black leather jacket and snug faded jeans, he was one of those men that radiated testosterone. And wasn't it just her luck, or lack of, that Michael Brandt, her jerk ex-husband's attorney was heading toward her holding her soda, sending her a dazzling smile that sent her stupid heart racing. She yanked the soda bottle out of his hand, thanked him and resisted the childish urge to kick him in the shin. Instead, she rushed out of the store.

She opened the back of the car to place the groceries inside. She pulled a Butterfinger bar out of one of the bags and got into the front seat. As she opened the candy bar, she glanced at Michael Brandt, still inside the store, who was now staring at her with an odd expression on his face, hands on his hips.

She heard movement in the back seat then felt something hard slam against her face. The candy bar flew out of her hand and landed on the floorboard.

"Drive."

She looked in the rearview mirror and gasped; a sliver of panic cut through her. A man in a black ski mask was slammed against her seat thrusting a gun in her face.

She punched the accelerator pitching gravel and dust in the parking lot. She screeched onto the road nearly sideswiping a pickup truck. Fear crushed her lungs and she could barely breathe.

"Turn right at the stop, Anne," he growled.

Christ, how did he know her name? She turned at the stop, her mind racing to remember what she had learned at her self-defense class. Stay calm. Stay calm and in control. Yeah, well that was a bit hard when there was a gun pressed to your cheek.

Calm down. She took a deep breath and tried to focus. She would not be this thug's victim. She would not.

What else did her self-defense teacher say? There was something about doing a 360-degree view of your surroundings when out alone. It was too late for that. She had stupidly forgotten that valuable piece of advice. She could jump from the car but it was going too fast.

Engage him in conversation. Wasn't that discussed in the class?

"Where are we going?"

"You'll know when we get there. I've got a private party in mind for just me and you."

Her stomach surged and she thought she might throw up. She had to do something. She had to do it *before* they reached his destination.

"Listen, I have my bank card with me. I could get you some cash."

"Shut up and keep driving."

Soon they would drive out of the residential area and be on country roads where houses and help would be out of reach. She looked in the rearview mirror again and noticed headlights. There was a truck behind her. She tapped on her brakes to get his attention.

"Stop hitting the brakes, bitch." The man in the ski mask turned around and seemed to notice the truck for the first time. He jabbed her again with the gun.

Frantic, she had to do something. Doing nothing could get her killed. Her mind went back to the self-defense class. Suddenly, she knew exactly what she must do.

She pressed the accelerator to speed up, scanning the right side of the road for what she needed. Turning a curve, she saw it standing near the road and aimed the car straight for it.

A sickening explosion of metal and glass assailed her ears as the car hit the tree on the passenger side. The air bag exploded, pinning her against her seat. The man in the ski mask flew over the seat into the front, pounding his head against the dashboard where he slumped.

The pain from the impact surged through her body but she fought it as she reached for the seat belt clasp. Once it was undone, she pulled the handle and pushed the door as hard as she could until it opened, sending her crashing to the ground. She must run. She must find help.

She staggered to her feet and tried to run, but her legs gave out after a couple of feet. She picked herself up and ran less than a block from the car, when she noticed someone running behind her. She could not let him catch her. He would kill her.

She dashed within a wooded area and ran as weeds, branches and thicket made long cuts on her legs. She ran until she felt her lungs would burst. She looked back and did not see the man.

She pushed ahead until she found a large tree and plastered her body behind it, willing herself to breathe. She listened, but heard nothing.

A large arm came out of nowhere, encircling her waist and trapping her against him. She fought, her fists pounding against his chest and kicking him until they both fell to the ground.

"Stop it. Anne, stop it. You're safe. I'm here to help you." He gripped her arms and pulled her to her feet. "Look at me. Do you remember me?"

He looked familiar. She pushed the tears and sweat from her eyes. Wildly, she looked up, searching his face. Michael Brandt? Confusion replaced the fear. "What are you doing here?"

"I followed you from the convenience store.

"We have to get back to the car," he added. "There is still a chance we can catch whoever did this to you." He used his flashlight to look her over for injuries. There was a wild look in her eyes he knew was shock, from his days as a cop. There were long, ugly scratches on her legs and arms, and a dark bruise was forming on her cheek. His eyes darkened as he thought of what he'd like to do to the bastard who did this to her.

"No, we can't go back there. He has a gun. He'll kill me," she sobbed.

"I'll protect you." He pulled her forward, his arm around her shoulders as he pushed through the trees and brush toward the road. She leaned against him, placing her arm around his waist. She felt a small gun inside the waistband of his jeans. She thought of grabbing it and forcing him to let her run away. But there was something in his voice that made her believe him. He would protect her.

She heard sirens and saw flashing lights. The police? She looked up at him.

"I called them from my cell. I saw the guy get in your car."

As they got closer, she saw the tangled metal mess that used to be her car. Her stomach tightened as her eyes scanned the area, looking for the man in the ski mask. He was not in the car. Two EMTs ran toward her, pulling her from Michael's arms, then leading her toward the ambulance. They made her sit in the back as they examined her. A small light pierced her eyes and a cuff tightened on her arm. Someone swabbed something on the cuts on her legs and arms.

She watched as officers searched her car and the surrounding areas. One of them led a German Shepherd that was sniffing the ground near the passenger side of her car. Michael Brandt was talking to an officer who looked like he was in charge. They talked as though they knew each other.

It was not cold but she began to shiver, her teeth chattering. She rubbed her temples. Her head was starting to throb.

"How is she?" She heard Michael's low voice as he talked to one of the EMTs.

"It wouldn't hurt if she went to the hospital to get checked out."

"I am *not* going to the hospital. I'm fine." She tried to get up, felt a sickening rush, and then sat back down.

Michael got into the ambulance then crouched down to her level to gaze at her face. He pulled off his leather jacket and placed it around her shoulders. He ran his thumb gently across her cheek where the bruise from the gun was darkening. He held her hand as he examined the long scratch on her arm, then leaned down to look at her legs.

"I told you. I'm fine."

He nodded at the officer standing near them she hadn't noticed until then. "This is Detective Smith. He needs to ask you some questions."

"So why were you at the convenience store after midnight?" Detective Smith took out a small notepad and pen.

"I've had one of the most seriously shitty days I've ever had and I was craving junk food."

"Did you notice the man who jumped in your car in the store?"

"No. I saw a store clerk and I bumped into Michael Brandt," she said gazing at Michael who nodded at the detective.

"How did the man get into your car?"

"I don't know. I had just put the groceries in the back of my SUV. I hadn't locked the doors yet. Suddenly, he appeared from the back seat."

"Did he have a weapon?"

"Yes. He had a gun."

"Did he say anything to you?"

"He told me to drive. I knew he would kill me if I didn't."

"What else do you remember about him?"

"He wore a black ski mask. I don't know about his clothes. They may have been dark. He wore gloves."

"What else?"

"He didn't want money. I offered to take him to my bank machine, but he didn't want money."

"He didn't want money?"

"No, and he called me by my name. He knew my name." Panic choked her as she remembered this. Christ, he knew her name.

Michael's brows drew together in a concerned frown as his eyes met the detective's. It sounded like this carjacking was planned. He must have followed her to the store, which meant he'd been watching her.

"Are you sure about that? Are you sure he called you by your name?" He scribbled in his notepad.

"Yes, I'm sure. That's not something I'd forget."

"Is anyone angry with you? Can you think of someone who would want to hurt you?"

"No," she said as she shook her head.

"I can," Michael interrupted. "Her divorce hearing was this morning and her ex-husband, Allan Long, was very pissed at her."

"It wasn't Allan. I would have recognized his voice."

"What did you have in the car besides your groceries?"

"My purse. I have a small yellow leather purse. Did you find it?"

"Yes, we found the purse but the contents are scattered around the car. Do you remember what was in the purse?"

"Why do you want to know what was in my purse?"

"I'm trying to determine if he took anything from the purse that might give him your address."

"Oh, crap."

"If you could see the contents, do you think you would remember anything that is missing?"

"Maybe."

In the back seat of her SUV, she saw a tube of lipstick, a brush, and a powder compact. In the front seat, she noticed her keys, cell phone, driver's license and a small makeup bag that contained her credit cards. She picked it up and looked inside, all cards were accounted for.

"Is anything missing?"

"Did you find a letter? There was a letter from my attorney about my hearing this morning."

"We'll look again, but no letter was found. Was the letter addressed to your home?"

"I can't remember if Stanley sent it to my home or office."

The detective looked at Michael with an expression that said "not good" then turned to Anne. If the carjacker didn't already know her address, he did now.

"That's all for now. If I were you, I'd listen to the EMTs and make a stop at the hospital to get checked out."

"No thanks. I just want to go home."

"Do you have someone to come get you to take you home?"

"*I'm* taking her home." Michael ignored her surprised expression, opened the back of her SUV and pulled out the bags of groceries. He led her to his truck by her arm, threw the groceries in the back and helped her inside.

"Listen, I can call a taxi or something."

"No, you're not."

"I can get a ride. You don't have to take me home."

"Yes, I do. I suddenly have this craving for junk food."

Chapter 2

When they pulled into her driveway, Michael insisted Anne stay in the car until he checked out the house. He pulled the gun out of his jeans and entered the house with her key. He moved from room to room, turning on lights as he went. By the time he came out to get her, the house was ablaze with lights and looked like someone was having a party.

"I appreciate your doing that, but I can take it from here." She moved to the back of the truck where Michael was retrieving the grocery bags. She was grateful for his help, but she hadn't forgotten he was Allan's attorney. Anne trusted him about as far as she could throw him, which considering his height and weight, was not very far.

"I may have saved your life tonight, the least you can do is offer me something to eat—which is why I was at that convenience store in the first place. I'm starving."

She followed him as he headed toward the house with the bags. Once inside, he strode to the kitchen and laid the groceries on the counter. He leaned back and let his eyes roam over her as she entered the room. She took off his jacket and laid it on the back of a chair. Her face was pale, and fatigue settled in pockets under her eyes. He shouldn't be thinking about how hot she looked, pale or not. He also shouldn't be thinking about what she'd be like in bed, but he was.

"There should be some water or a bottle of wine in the fridge," she offered. "Help yourself; I'm going to clean up a bit."

Once she was in the bathroom, she looked in the mirror. The

darkening bruise across her cheek was going to be a doozy. She turned to the shower and began running hot water until the room was warm and steamy.

Michael looked in her refrigerator and decided it was pretty sorry. For food, there was a half-eaten container of yogurt, eggs, some butter and not much else. She was definitely overdue for a grocery run. He found the wine she'd mentioned and a half dozen bottles of water. He pulled wine glasses from the cabinet, filled them and set them at the table. He could hear the shower running and tried not to let his imagination run sexual. He opened the salsa jar and tortilla chips then put them on the table. Then he noticed the ice cream and put it in her freezer.

He looked around the room. Nice kitchen. He liked the white cabinets with the dark granite counters as well as the stainless steel appliances. She must be a neat freak. No dishes in the sink, countertops were glowing and everything was neatly in its place. He noticed a cabinet above the sink with beveled glass doors filled with a few bottles of wine, a small bottle of rum, a pina colada mix, and a six pack of wine coolers.

The shower stopped. He could hear her moving about, opening and closing cabinet doors. He leaned back against the sink. The door opened and she moved down the hall and into the kitchen. His dark eyes roamed over her. Her hair was wet and she'd changed into a thick terrycloth robe. She still looked very hot so he tried to divert his attention.

"Where's your dog?"

She followed his eyes to the large dog bowl near the back door.

"He's at the vet. He's been sick to his stomach and he's getting checked out."

He remembered his manners, pulled a chair out and invited her to sit down. He sniffed a sweet flowery scent as she sat down. She smelled like a mixture of roses and woman, and it spiked his temperature up a couple of notches. If he didn't get his mind off sex, he would soon have an embarrassing and noticeable problem.

She had hoped he would choose the chair farthest from her, but he chose the nearest one, sitting so close she could feel the warmth of his long legs. Her senses went on alert.

Annoyed with him or not, she noticed his rugged good looks and the way his black

T-shirt stretched across his muscles. She breathed in his musky, male scent and felt a buzz of sexual awareness. She lifted her glass and downed some wine.

He poured the chips into a large bowl he found, and then pulled it toward them, along with the salsa. She didn't think it was much food if he was really hungry, but she'd be damned if she'd cook for him. She just wanted him to leave. She finished her glass of wine and he poured another.

"What kind of dog?"

"Giant Schnauzer. His name is Harley and he's very smart. In fact, I think he is more human than dog." She smiled for the first time since he met her.

"I like dogs. I used to have a Lab as a kid. I always thought I would get a dog someday, but things are always so busy at work, I doubt I'd have much time to spend with him." He noticed her tense when he referred to his "work" and silently cursed himself for bringing it up. So he changed the subject.

"So the guy who carjacked you knew your name. Was there anything familiar about him?"

"I keep thinking about him. Have I seen his eyes before? Have I heard his voice? I just don't know."

"The detectives are going to pull up the surveillance tape at the convenience store. If we're lucky, they'll get a hit and identify him."

He finished his wine, stood up and helped her clean off the table. She looked so tired it tugged at his heart.

"Come walk me to the door, then lock up and go to sleep. You look beat."

She led him to the front door and opened it. He stood there for a moment looking down at her. An impulse came over him. He could blame it on the wine, the adrenaline or the situation. But it was something he'd wanted to do since he first laid eyes on her. He shouldn't do it. He had to do it.

He pulled her to him and kissed her slowly and gently. At first, she stiffened and didn't move. Then he felt her lean toward him on the tips of her toes, her hands moving up his chest.

His kiss tasted so good she wanted to drink him in. The mixture of wine and man was intoxicating as his tongue flicked inside the recesses of her mouth. She breathed in his warm male scent. She should stop him, but instead she pressed closer to him wanting more.

He stopped, leaned back and looked down at her. Her eyes registered want, confusion, and then anger before she stepped back.

"If you think you're going to get lucky because you helped me tonight, you're wrong. Contrary to whatever Allan may have told you, I am not a big fan of thank you sex *or* any other kind of casual sex. Good night."

She pushed him through the open door and shut it soundly behind him. She locked the door, then leaned against it closing her eyes, still feeling lust surging through her veins.

What was with this guy? He represents her ex during one of the worst moments of her life, probably saved her life, and then delivers one of the hottest kisses she's ever experienced at her front door. All in one day.

For that matter, what was wrong with her? She knew nothing about him, other than he represented her jerk of an ex-husband. Yet she couldn't remember a time when she was more attracted to a man. She chalked up her reaction to his kiss to the wine, the surge of adrenaline, or the fact she hadn't been with a man for over a year, and could be going through some serious withdrawal.

There was a hammer pounding and it was louder than the painful one in her head. She pulled her pillow over her head and moaned. Damn it. What was that noise? She stuck out an arm to search for her clock radio. What time was it anyway? She rolled over and landed on the floor with a resounding thud. Crap, she was in the living room on the sofa. She remembered now. After hours of tossing and turning in her bed upstairs, she'd grabbed a pillow and her grandma's quilt and camped out in the living room close to the front door. The hammer continued to pound and she realized someone was at her front door.

She cursed, got to her feet then looked out the window to see who was at her door. Damn.

"Are you crazy? What time is it? What are you doing here?"

Michael looked her over noting she was wearing a short knit shirt and plaid pajama shorts then pushed past her carrying three takeout bags. Not a morning person, he decided. He looked at his watch.

"It's 7:15 and I brought breakfast." He headed toward the kitchen, leaving her at the door with her mouth open.

She rubbed her eyes and asked herself is she was having a dream. She plodded down the hall in her bare feet, realizing that every muscle in her body was signaling some level of pain. She gritted her teeth and watched him empty the bags.

"I don't recall ordering the Michael Brandt breakfast home delivery service." Sarcasm threaded through her voice as she leaned against the door frame.

He responded by pushing a hot cup of coffee in her hand and pushing her toward a chair.

"I didn't know what you liked so I ordered some of everything. There are pancakes, scrambled eggs, bacon, breakfast sandwiches, and muffins." He listed each item as he took them from the bags and set it on the table. He pulled a couple of plates from the cabinet then pulled silverware from the drawer.

She watched him over the rim of her coffee cup. Thank God for coffee, she thought as the caffeine kicked in.

"I'm not hungry," she said as she watched him dig in.

"Yes, you are. Eat something." He had a look in his eyes that dared her not to eat, so she picked at the scrambled eggs.

"You look like crap this morning." His dark eyes did a full assessment of her injuries from the now dark-purple bruise across her cheek, to the reddened cuts and scratches on her arms and legs.

"Tell me what you really think." She hadn't looked in the mirror but she knew he was probably right. Everything hurt, and now there was a circle of throbbing pain at her ribs.

He moved to crouch down in front of her and lifted her top to reveal a stretch of black and blue bruises. "Bet this is from the seat belt." She slapped his hand then smoothed her top down.

"Calm down. I'm not trying to jump you." He held her leg up, examining the cuts on her legs. She jerked when he ran his finger over a bruise. "You should have gone to the hospital. They would have given you something for pain."

"I'm fine. I'll take some aspirin."

He moved back to the table and ate a couple of bacon strips while he stared at her.

"What?"

"I'm just wondering why you hit the tree. Your car was not out of control."

"Self Defense 101. If your attacker is on the passenger side of the car, slam into something on that side to disable him. So I hit the tree on his side of the car." She leaned back, thinking about the impact, the glass and metal, and she shuddered. But she'd done the right thing. If she hadn't hit that tree, there was a good chance she wouldn't be alive today. Her only regret was that her attacker wasn't hurt seriously enough to be caught.

His brows raised and he looked at her with a new respect. That was a smart thing to do. And how she could think straight, with this jerk shoving a gun in her face, forcing her to drive, was nothing short of amazing.

A muscle flicked angrily at his jaw as he thought about her attacker, and what he'd like to do to the guy if he was ever caught. The bastard better think twice about going near her again. Which is why he slept in his truck outside her house last night. He didn't believe for a minute that her carjacking was random. There was a good chance the prick would try to get at her again, and Michael wanted to be there if he tried.

He looked at her again and fought the urge to pull her into his lap and kiss her until she forgot about the attacker and everything else. He decided she would probably scratch his eyes out if he did, so Michael dumped the idea.

She was in pain. He could see it in her eyes, whether she'd admit it or not. He got up, walked down the hall into the bathroom, and opened the medicine cabinet. He retrieved a bottle of aspirin and returned to the kitchen, placing it in front of her.

She slipped a couple into her mouth and downed them with the last of her coffee. She moved to her coffee maker to make more. She got a bag of Godiva Chocolate Crème coffee out of the cabinet then turned to Michael, scoop in hand.

"You haven't answered my question. Why are you here?"

"Your car looked like it was totaled, and the crime techs may have it for weeks, even if it isn't. I thought I'd give you a drive to get a rental. You're going to need a car, right?"

"Nice of you to offer, but I can handle that myself." She leaned against the counter and tried to give him her best I-can-take-care-of-myself-thank-you expression. She considered his glare and decided it wasn't working.

"You've got thirty minutes to get ready. I'll make more coffee." He took the coffee scoop out of her hand and pushed her toward the bathroom.

Forty minutes later, they were headed down Route 40 looking for car rentals. Anne distracted herself by checking out the man next to her. He was still wearing the black

T-shirt and jeans he had on the night before. She couldn't figure out his sport, but he looked athletic, his muscled arms straining against the fabric of his shirt. He definitely worked out. A navy jacket, blue shirt, grey pants and matching paisley tie hung in the back. Her mind went back to last night's kiss, the feel of his hard chest under her hands, and she flushed with the memory.

"Are you checking me out?" He looked at her with a smug grin plastered across his face.

"No, are you serious?" She rolled her eyes, then looked out the window so he could not see her grin.

"I know a place up the road that can help you out with a car." He drove a bit further then drove in to a Honda new car dealership.

"What are you doing? I thought we were going to a rental place."

"I know the dealer here. He can take care of it."

As they got closer to the building, she noticed a man in a white shirt and jeans walking toward them as if he expected them. He waved and smiled. Michael got out of the truck and shook hands with the man. They had a short conversation, and then Michael walked to her side of the car, opened the door and helped her get out. The man introduced himself as the car dealer and extended his hand to Anne.

"I bet you're Anne. I've got something for you." He led her to a brand-new, blue Honda CRV, the updated version of her SUV. Confused she looked at Michael then the dealer.

"I'm confused. I'm looking for a rental."

"This is it," said the dealer as he flashed a brilliant smile at her. "You can rent it until you get your insurance check. Then you can decide if you want to buy this one or another one."

Something buzzed and Michael pulled his cell phone out of his pocket and walked back toward the truck to talk.

She peered inside the car. This was definitely the luxury model and not the standard, stripped-down model she had. The seats were beige leather and a navigation system was mounted in the center of the dash. The audio system was jacked up and a power moon roof was carved in the ceiling.

"How much is it a month?"

"Don't worry about it. It's taken care of. Just hoping you'll want to buy it when you get your check."

She frowned, squinting her eyes at him then looked back at Michael, who was still talking on his cell.

"What's going on? What do you mean, 'it's taken care of?" She didn't know what was going on, but if this was a favor or charity, she didn't like it.

"Anne, you're starting to insult me," he said, avoiding her questions. "I own this dealership and I can do whatever I want. If I want to loan you a car, knowing you'll probably buy it when you get your insurance check, that's good business. Do you want it or not?"

Michael followed Anne in her new SUV in his truck as they left the lot. He rolled down his window and gave a thumbs-up to the dealer as they passed. There were times when being a defense attorney wasn't so bad, like when a client with a car dealership owed him a lot of money he didn't have.

Weeks passed, and although she kept calling, she got little information from the police about the carjacking. That was because they had nothing. The attacker wore a ski mask and gloves. The convenience store surveillance tape revealed nothing.

No prints either. He wore gloves. If he had injuries when she crashed the car, he didn't bleed, because the crime techs found no fluids to test for DNA. No hair. No fibers. Nothing. It was like he was never there.

Michael had called a couple of times, but she had skillfully avoided him, thanks to Caller ID. She thought she saw his silver Escalade EXT pass her house a couple of times, but she had to be mistaken, because he lived on the other side of town. She knew because she'd Googled him.

She finally sold the house and gave Allan the money. Her partner at her computer company argued with her for days about selling her share of the business. She'd sold it anyway. It was worth it to get Allan out of her life.

The moving company representative called at seven o'clock to say the moving team had arrived at Golden Acres Farm and were unloading her things.

Anne smiled as she heard Daisy in the background giving orders and skillfully guiding the movers so that her things were in the right place. The petite blonde in her late forties had run the Golden Acres household for ten years. Anne thought of her as another gift from Marion. Daisy Brooks had been Marion's best friend since childhood. When Daisy's husband died unexpectedly, leaving her with more bills than money, Marion invited her to live on the farm. Daisy demonstrated such a talent for running the household that Marion let her take over. Over the years, Daisy's supportive nature and affection had earned her a special place in Anne's heart.

Anne's black Giant Schnauzer, Harley was 75 pounds of shivering anticipation when he noticed her suitcases packed and sensed a trip was in order. He'd received a good bill of health from his vet and was back to his hyperactive self. He raced down the stairs ahead of her, nearly tripping her in the process. She opened the passenger side of the SUV and he bounded inside.

Once they were on their way, she smiled at Harley, who was sitting in the passenger seat as if he were a person. It's a good thing he can't drive, she thought. He is so excited they'd get a speeding ticket for sure.

It was a two-hour drive, but she didn't mind. It gave her time to think. She looked at herself in the rear-view mirror. The dark bruise that marked her cheek had faded, and the scratches and cuts on her arms and legs had healed. The attack had resulted in one good thing: it made her more aware of her surroundings, more careful. The bad thing was she couldn't get the attack out of her mind, and she' become jumpy and a bit paranoid.

Her post-divorce feelings of anger were dissipating. She had regained her strength as each day passed. The gloss returned to her golden-streaked auburn hair, as did the rosy warmth in her cheeks. The woman reflected in the mirror was a new one, a stronger one. For the first time in a long time, Anne felt alive.

Marion was right when she said Anne loved the farm as much as she did. Some of her favorite memories were weekends on the farm with Marion. She loved the quiet evenings sitting on the porch swing, watching the sunset as she sipped wine and talked with Marion. God, she missed her. Marion was more of a mother than her own had ever been.

It wasn't long until the farm came into view, Golden Acres Farm, 300 acres of the most fertile farm land in the state of Indiana. She turned into the long driveway and sighed. She was home. The farm was the home she had yearned for as a child. It was a wonderful gift she would always cherish.

Whimsical in design and painted light rose with burgundy trim, the house was a Victorian Queen Anne built near the turn of the century. Anne smiled as she remembered the way Marion lovingly maintained it to keep its original glory. A wrap-around porch that graced the front of the house was lined with white wicker chairs, tables and a porch swing. Anne remembered the many hot summer evenings when she and Marion would talk for hours on the porch, appreciating a breeze and each other.

Anne let an excited and barking Harley out of the car. As he raced around the house, Daisy flew out the front door, smiling and waving until she reached Anne with a hug so tight it almost took her breath away.

"It is so good to see you." Daisy said. "I know you are going to be happy here, Anne. I just know it. Marion knew it, too."

Harley bounded from the edge of the house, noticed Daisy, and nearly knocked her down.

"I don't know what he loves more—me, or the dog biscuits I give him!" Daisy laughed.

"I know the feeling." Anne said.

"Let's go inside. I've got a pot of your favorite coffee and some cinnamon rolls fresh from the oven. Let's celebrate your homecoming. You come too, Harley!"

The kitchen was large and filled with vintage mahogany cabinets. A stone fireplace graced one wall. The appliances were modern and the counters were smoky granite, thanks to a renovation Marion did a couple of years earlier. It was a warm, welcoming room with a large window that faced the gardens in back.

Daisy gave Harley a dog biscuit, then delivered two cups of steamy coffee. She went back for two plates of the cinnamon rolls she had just pulled from the oven.

"If you keep feeding me like this, I'm going to have to run extra miles." Anne teased as she pulled the roll apart with her fingers, savoring every bite.

"Oh, please. A couple of cinnamon rolls are not going to push you over the edge to obesity."

When she heard the kitchen door close, she turned to see Hank Anderson, holding his baseball cap in his large hands, enter the room. He was a short, wiry man who had worked as Marion's farm foreman for almost five years. Anne was pleased when he agreed to stay on to work for her after Marion passed away.

"Hi, Hank. Good to see you. Why don't you sit down and have some of Daisy's amazing coffee? There are cinnamon rolls, too."

"Don't mind if I do. I could smell those rolls from the barn." He walked to the sink to wash his hands. He moved to the table and watched Daisy pour his coffee and plunk a couple of rolls on a plate, then looked at Anne. "I saw Harley in the yard. He looks like he's grown a foot since last I saw him."

"They don't stay puppies for long, do they?"

"No, they certainly don't."

"Have you thought more about the wind technology project I mentioned last week?"

"I've thought about it, but I am not sure I like the idea of some developer putting some of those giant steel monsters on Golden Acres. Maybe I'm old-fashioned, but I just can't see it."

"Hank, it's an opportunity to build more revenue for the farm. Our finances are certainly in the black, but too close to the red to make me comfortable."

"I understand. I guess I was hoping we'd do something more traditional like adding more livestock."

"We can discuss that, but I want to talk to one of the wind technology developers, too, Hank."

"You're the boss." There was an edge to his tone. "I need to get back to work now." He put his cup in the sink, thanked Daisy, and left the room through the kitchen door.

"That went well," Anne said sarcastically.

"When it comes to farming, Hank is set in his ways," said Daisy. She watched him walk to the barn where he stood talking to a few of the farm hands. "I've overheard him talking with the farm hands about wind technology and he is even less in favor of it than he told you just now."

"I don't understand why he would be opposed. Wind power is an opportunity to create clean electricity, and we benefit with increased revenue. I'm going to move ahead after I do more Internet research on the topic."

"Here is your mail and our local newspaper." Daisy said, changing the subject. "You'll find something interesting in the local section."

Anne turned to the local section and was surprised to see her photo. "Seriously? I can't believe someone thought my moving to the farm was newsworthy."

"Honey, it isn't every day when a female-owned farm is passed on to another female. Marion was considered one of the most successful women in the county. So it's natural that people are interested in the woman who is taking her place."

Daisy poured more coffee in their cups as Anne turned the paper to the front page. There was a picture of a pretty college student who was missing. Frowning, Anne looked at Daisy, "Did you know about this?"

"Yes, she disappeared about a month ago while walking to one of her college classes. The whole community has pulled together on this one, planning searches and posting flyers. Her parents are beside themselves with fear and worry. You might remember Ruth Mitchell. She sometimes came out for tea with Marion. Rachel is her daughter."

"I think I met Ruth once. Isn't she a first grade teacher at the elementary?"

"Yes. Rachel is her only child. Poor woman, my heart goes out to her."

"Daisy, let's hope for the best, but in the meantime please find out if there is anything we can do to help. I'm going to check out the gardens." She pushed her coffee and empty plate aside and moved toward the back door. She wanted to spend some quiet time in the back yard before she tackled those moving boxes.

The late summer gardens of Golden Acres Farms were lush with both flowers and vegetables. A sweep of green hostas pressed against the house, and a plot of rose bushes of every type lay before Anne, enticing her with their soft, sweet fragrance. She sat in the garden on a wrought iron bench and leaned down to smell the sweet, rich fragrance of a dark pink and yellow Peace rose. It was her favorite, pale yellow petals with pink edges. She smiled as she enjoyed the quiet, gentle breeze that caressed her skin. Yes, she thought, moving here was a good decision.

Harley appeared with a bright yellow tennis ball wedged between his teeth, his tail wagging in anticipation.

"Any chance you'd like to play catch?" He dropped the ball at her feet and ran several feet away, eagerly waiting for her to toss the ball. Laughing, she threw the ball and watched him leap to catch it mid-air.

He sipped his coffee and studied Anne from the kitchen window, while Daisy talked to the movers in the hallway. Anne's hair was tied in a high pony tail and flowed down the back of her snug blue T-shirt in soft waves. She tossed the ball for the large dog with strength that was at odds with the slenderness of her body. Her lips were full and sexy, her eyes under a flutter of thick lashes were dark blue, if he remembered correctly. She had a face that would make a man look twice. Okay, more than twice. He kept his gaze on her. All he could think about is what it would be like to pull her hard against his chest and kiss that full, sexy mouth again.

Daisy sidled up to stand next to him and refilled his empty coffee cup. "I know what you're thinking."

"Mind reader, are you?"

"From what I hear, you've got plenty of women in town to capture your attention."

"You shouldn't believe all you hear, Daisy."

"Anne's been through hell the past few years. I don't want to see her get hurt again."

"You mean her divorce?"

"Anne has a history of losing people she loves, starting from her childhood. Her grandmother raised her when her parents left her so they could travel. Losing her grandmother last year hit her hard. It wasn't long after that Marion died. Marion was the mother Anne never had. And less than six months after Marion, she lost the baby she was carrying—the one that bastard Allan Long didn't want."

"Damn, you're right. She's been through hell."

"If there's even a small chance you might hurt her, please stay away. If you hurt her, you'll have me to answer to." Daisy's dark eyes held a seriousness he had not seen before.

Anne threw the ball until her arm began to ache. "Let's play later, big boy. I've got unpacking to do." As she neared the back door to the kitchen, she overheard Daisy talking with someone. She heard a man say he had to go to his car for his briefcase, then Daisy said she'd warm his coffee. By the time she entered the room, Daisy had her back to her, pouring the steamy brew in a cup.

"Did I hear a man's voice?"

Before Daisy could answer, a large man filled the doorframe. His ruggedly handsome face was familiar as he smiled at Anne. "Hello." His voice was deep and masculine, but there was gentleness about it.

Michael Brandt? Confused she looked from Michael to Daisy. What was he doing in her kitchen?

"Honey, sit down. You look like you've just seen a ghost." Daisy exclaimed. "What's wrong?"

Before she could respond, Michael rushed to a chair, pulling it out for her then pushing it forward as she sat.

"Michael, I'd like to introduce you to…"

"Anne and I know each other." The familiarity in his tone implicated they had been on friendly terms for years. This was certainly not the case.

She grinned tightly at him as he sat down.

Daisy read the annoyance in Anne's expression, and then made an excuse to leave the two alone.

"I have the carjacking report. They're not closing the case, but there isn't much to go on." He took a gulp of his coffee.

"Why didn't the detective bring it?"

"I volunteered because I knew I would be in the neighborhood."

"You volunteered? Why would you be in this neighborhood?" She took a quick, sharp breath.

Michael ignored her questions. "I live near here. Didn't Daisy tell you I'm your closest neighbor?" He leaned down to pet Harley, who had planted himself beside Michael's chair. "By the way, welcome to the neighborhood."

My closest neighbor, Anne thought. Well, so much for thinking of the farm as her oasis. How could it be an oasis when Allan's attorney was sitting in her kitchen and was living as her closest neighbor?

Changing the subject, Anne said, "How can you live out here and have a legal practice in Indianapolis? That's a two-hour drive each way."

"I dissolved my law practice. I bought the farm a couple of months ago. Didn't move in until last weekend. I've got a job thing in the works here."

"What's that mean?"

"That's a story for another time. I have a meeting in town in about fifteen minutes and I'm sure you have a lot of unpacking to do. Maybe you could show me out?"

Anne wanted to tell him 'you found your way in here, find your way out.' But she bit her tongue. She could be civil. After all, he did come to her rescue when she was carjacked; not to mention that time at the bar parking lot.

Instantly Michael was at her side, holding the chair for her. She led him through the house, with his hand planted firmly against the small of her back, sending tiny involuntary tremors up her spine. Once outside, he leaned against his silver metallic Escalade EXT parked in her driveway.

She was lovelier than he remembered. It had been a couple of weeks since he'd seen her. He couldn't stop thinking about her—and he had tried. He had to see her again.

He tilted her head up and rubbed the pad of his thumb against the bruise that was fading on her cheek. "This looks better. How about the rest?"

"Good. Everything is fine." Lie. She still couldn't sleep through the night. She consistently awoke from the same nightmare when she saw the attacker's ski-masked face and the gun at her cheek. His gaze lingered on her eyes, and she realized he knew she was lying.

"If you ever want to talk, have dinner or something." He reached out to push a stray strand of hair from her eyes.

"Not a good idea." She backed up a step. Is he insane? He may think he rescued her but he also Allan's attorney. Why on earth would she want to see him again? Being Allan's attorney was a good reason not to see him; but not the main reason, which was the way he made her feel just by being close. She couldn't look at the man without getting itchy. Too long without a man will do that to you.

His eyebrows went up. Not a good idea? He stared at her for a moment, got in his truck, pushed it in gear and headed to the road. There was nothing he liked more than a challenge. This particular challenge had been planted in his brain for weeks.

Anne watched him leave and muttered "damn him" and a few other expletives. She was so filled with annoyance that she didn't notice Daisy standing beside her.

"Good looking, strong, muscular as in ripped body, nice ass and smart to boot. There isn't much not to like, is there, Anne?" Daisy said, as she watched his car until it disappeared.

"There's *plenty* not to like, starting with the fact he's Allan's attorney." Anne frowned with exasperation.

"I heard he's got half the women in town fawning over him."

"That's *their* problem," Anne said, rolling her eyes.

"He bought the Hastings farm when Sam Hastings died. He's visited a couple of times. Seems like a good man. I think he'll make a good neighbor."

Well there's the bitch now. He slowed the old Mustang to a stop and pulled binoculars from the glove box so he could focus on her in the distance. Yes, that was definitely her. He'd seen her picture in the newspaper. That's how he found her. She had that smug look about her in the photo. Not like the freaked-out expression she had in the car when she noticed his gun.

Anne Mason was just another bitch who thought she was smarter and better. Just like the one in his trunk. Poor little college tramp. All tied up and nowhere to go. He'd show her a thing or two she hadn't learned in college. He owed her that much for what she'd done to him. And one day he'd show Anne Mason a thing or two, starting with a little gift of a corpse.

Chapter 3

Anne parked her SUV in front of the Wright Wind Technologies, Inc. offices. She pulled down her visor to check her look in the mirror.

She determined there must be no question at this meeting that she was a competent businesswoman who looked and acted like one. Early in her career, her mentor had taught her how to dress for the best negotiating stance. Dressing like you mean business usually meant you got it.

She touched up her pink lip gloss then scanned the rest of her appearance. Her go-to business look was lightweight wool-blend pantsuit in burgundy. The fabric had just enough give to complement her curves. She wanted to project business, but had no wish to look like a man.

Wright Wind Technologies, Inc., headed by Dan Wright, offered an opportunity for Golden Acres Farm to gain revenue from allowing developers like Dan to install large wind turbines on her land. He'd contacted her several times, but she put him off until she could do a thorough Internet research on wind technology in general, as well as his company specifically.

The receptionist led her into a small conference room with large posters lining its walls. Anne was early, so she laid her black leather briefcase on the conference table and walked the room examining the wind power posters on the wall.

Dan Wright didn't know what to expect when he first laid eyes on Anne Mason, but had to admit he was pleasantly surprised. She was a knock-out with sun-streaked auburn hair to her shoulders, lightly tanned skin, and the bluest eyes he had ever seen. She certainly didn't look like any of the other farmers he worked with.

He ran his fingers through his sandy hair then cleared his throat to get her attention, extending his hand to shake hers as she moved closer.

"Hi, you must be Anne Mason. Thanks for agreeing to meet with me today," he said. Dan pulled out a chair at the conference table. "Please have a seat. Would you like some coffee?"

"No, thank you. I'm eager to talk business."

"Tell me what you already know about wind power, so I don't give you a lot of information you don't need."

"I know that wind power is a clean electricity resource that is generated by capturing the wind's energy by those giant wind mills or turbines I can see when driving on I-65 in Northwest Indiana."

"I'm impressed. You've done your homework," Dan said.

"I suspect you've done your homework too. Why are you interested in Golden Acres for wind farm development?"

"We did some preliminary testing and discovered your land has average wind speeds of 18 miles per hour at 33 feet. Along with easy access to transmission lines, this indicates that your land is suitable for wind farm development, so we are interested in leasing some of your acreage."

"Depending on the revenue, I have twenty acres that I would consider leasing. But I need some more specifics about the lease—especially what is required on our end."

"Anne, one of your responsibilities in the lease is to provide a permanent service road so that our people can work on each wind turbine if needed. You will also need to commit to keep that service road clear no matter what the weather."

"That's not a problem. Would we be able to plant crops or have livestock on the acreage where the wind turbines would stand?"

"Yes, you would. In addition, the impact on wildlife is minimal."

"Good. What kind of revenue are we talking about?"

"We can offer you $3,500 per year for each turbine. So if you commit twenty acres with four wind turbines on each acre, you can make $280,000 per year."

"If you can make that $5,000 per turbine per year, you've got a deal."

She watched him push back in his chair as he stared at her. No doubt he was surprised that she asked for more money, and she hoped she hadn't asked for too much.

"Anne, you drive a hard bargain. I need to run that past my team, and I will let you know the answer before the end of the week."

Dan walked her to her car and watched as she drove away. He wouldn't mind mixing business and pleasure with Anne Mason. No, he wouldn't mind at all.

The man leaned against the building across the street and took another drag of his cigarette before he tossed it to the sidewalk. Anne Mason had proven harder to stalk than the others.

Her movements to and from the farm were unpredictable, so last week he'd put himself at risk and broke into her house to install monitoring software on her computer. The installation took about 20 seconds, so he was in and out of the unlocked farm house and into the cornfield on his way to his car before the housekeeper finished sweeping the living room rug downstairs.

He remembered laughing once he reached his car. Anne Mason thought she was so freaking smart, but apparently not smart enough. You gotta love digital age technology. From his home computer, he was now reading her every chat and email conversation. He'd known about her meeting with Dan Wright since last week. Yes, she was much easier to shadow now.

He was overjoyed to learn from an email her housekeeper would soon be out-of-town. The fewer people surrounding Anne Mason, the easier it would be for him to get her in his possession. And then the party would begin. She'd learn there were consequences for what she did to him—rather deadly consequences.

By the time Anne reached the athletic track of the elementary school, it was already 6:00 p.m. The track was a fourth of a mile, so Anne determined she'd run eight laps to make the two-mile goal she set for herself. She pulled off her light blue sweatpants, revealing matching running shorts beneath. She pulled a hair band from her pocket and bound her long, auburn hair into a ponytail before she warmed up, bending from her waist to stretch until her hands touched the rough surface of the cinder track.

The September air was crisp but she would barely notice the chill after a lap or two. She began running in place, her long legs moving in rhythm.

Dan Wright had called her within an hour of their meeting and agreed to her request for $5,000 per year for each wind turbine set up on Golden Acres land, which would amount to additional revenue of $400,000 per year. Once she completed this celebratory run, she'd go home to tell Hank and Daisy. This was such good news.

A silver-haired man slowly jogged past her, openly appraising her from head-to-toe. She'd seen him on the track before and each time he'd eyed her like she was a chocolate chip cookie fresh from the oven. He had the annoying habit of disregarding her back-the-hell-off glares.

She ignored him and began running her laps, passing him easily as she shot forward. A man in a black baseball cap wearing mirrored sunglasses and a black hooded sweatshirt sat in the bleachers smoking a cigarette. There was something about him that made her uncomfortable. He appeared to be focused on *her* but thanks to the mirrored sunglasses, she couldn't be certain. She shrugged and chastised herself for having an overactive imagination.

Heaven knows, since her carjacking she had lost her sense of trust and gained an extreme and unreasonable suspicion of other people and their motives. She spent more time looking in her rearview mirror than watching the road ahead. She'd even become suspicious of men she caught looking at her, asking herself if each could be the carjacker. She'd talked to Detective Smith last week and though he had no new information, he'd emphasized he didn't think the carjacking was random. So if it was planned, who was watching her movements and wanted to hurt her, or worse? Allan was furious with her, but would he hurt her? Was he the kind of person who would hire someone to do it for him?

A tall, muscular man in a hooded gray sweatshirt sprinted past her on lap two. His powerful thighs and legs were tan and covered with fine hair. His muscular body was lean but athletic, she noted. He looked to be about 6'5" and around 230 pounds. The hood on his sweatshirt covered his head so she couldn't get a good look at his face. Anne's curiosity peaked. She'd been running on the track for over a month and there was a group of runners she thought of as regulars. She hadn't seen him before. She quickened her pace to get a glimpse of his face, but he was running too fast for her to catch up with him. He was already past the starting point while she was just a little over half-way there.

The darkening sky triggered the automatic lighting system that submerged the track in light. She noticed the silver-haired man and two other joggers had finished their laps and were leaving the track through the heavy gate at the tall chain-link fence that surrounded the track. The man in the mirrored sunglasses on the bleachers was gone.

A flock of Canadian geese, flying in a V formation in the late afternoon sky, caught Anne's eye and made her a little sad. Winter will arrive soon, she thought, and her running days would cease until spring unless she could find a good indoor facility. This far away from the city made that possibility unlikely at best.

A sudden breeze whipped at her hair, tugging tendrils loose from her ponytail. She was nearing her fourth lap, was winded, but holding up. Running made her feel lithe and full of energy. The run energized her as much as coming out the winner of the wind farm negotiations.

Running was a good activity to drive Michael from her thoughts. Lately that accomplishment was a feat in itself. He was making weekly, sometimes bi-weekly visits to the farm. He called on Daisy one week to ask her to help him interview a housekeeper. The next week, he spoke to Hank about a farmhand he needed. Whatever the excuse for the visit, he would seek her out whether she was working in the rose garden, playing with Harley or working on her computer in her office. It was becoming hard for her to be annoyed with someone who was so damned good looking and charming. But remembering he was her ex-husband's attorney reminded her of at least one good reason to distrust him.

The man in the gray sweatshirt passed her again, his shoes pounding the cinder surface. But this time, he slowed his speed once he was several feet ahead of her. Soon he was jogging beside her. As she turned to look at him, he jerked down the hood to his sweatshirt with a mischievous smile that sent shockwaves through her system.

"Michael?" Her shocked expression quickly turned to irritation as she hastened her speed. He easily kept up with her, barely winded while her own lungs seemed ready to burst. Her heart tripped wildly against her ribs more by his presence than physical exertion.

"What are you doing here?" She demanded.

"I stopped at the farm and Daisy told me you would be here." He shot her a smile that had her pulse racing. "I loaded her luggage in her car for her trip."

Anne nodded. She'd forgotten Daisy was leaving for a visit with her sister. They slowed to a walk. Several minutes passed before either of them spoke.

"You know they still haven't found Rachel Mitchell. The police think she was abducted." Michael said referring to the missing college student.

"So I read."

"It's been more than three months, so it's not likely she is alive."

"Why are you telling me this?" She said as she considered the quick and disturbing thought.

"Whoever abducted Rachel is still out there." He paused for a second then went on. "You really should be more careful about your safety. What are you doing out here alone?" Damn it. Did he just say that out loud? This guard-dog need to protect her or anyone else was foreign to him, and he didn't know what to do with it.

"I can take care of myself."

Michael caught her arm stopping her. "Seriously? I bet Rachel Mitchell thought she could take care of herself too."

Defiant, she threw her head back. "Am I supposed to melt because you're suddenly all protective? I'm not sure how other women react to that move, but it's lost on me."

Anne yanked her arm out of his grasp and pushed forward. Her left ankle gave way, sending her crashing down to the cinder track. She landed with a thud on her side, and a lightning bolt of pain shot up from her ankle.

She moaned and was aware of Michael's large hands touching her body as he gently turned her over to inspect her injuries. He carefully unlaced her shoe and removed it, along with her sock. She shrieked as he prodded her ankle and foot with his fingers.

"Easy, honey. I know it hurts." His voice was soothing and did not reveal the cold knot in his stomach when he saw the extent of her injuries. The entire right side of her leg was scraped and bleeding with dark bits of cinder embedded in her flesh.

She tried to rise to inspect the injuries for herself, but he gently—yet firmly—pushed Anne back down. Her ankle was throbbing violently now. Michael handed her back the shoe, effortlessly scooped her up in his arms, and began walking.

"Put me down," she cried weakly.

"Hell, no. You can't walk on that foot," he growled.

"Where are you taking me?" Whatever his answer, she was in too much pain to argue. She gazed up at his face, and then laid her head on his shoulder, trying to ignore the pain shooting up her leg, and the trip of her heartbeat at his nearness.

"I'm taking you to my truck, then to the hospital. This time you're going. You need to be seen by a doctor. Your ankle may be broken. I think the scrapes on your leg will need cleaned out, too." He reached his truck, opened the passenger door, and carefully placed Anne inside.

Once they reached the hospital emergency room, Anne was given an injection for pain, and Michael was banished from the room so she could be examined. In minutes, the injection took hold. The white-coated doctor became blurry and the room began to spin. Anne was became very sleepy, and darkness engulfed her.

Three hours later, she weakly opened her eyes to find a nurse taking her pulse.

"Hello, sleepyhead. You missed all the excitement." The nurse smiled down at her and patted her arm. "We cleaned out the cuts and scrapes on your legs and took some x-rays of your ankle." She held a tiny flashlight to Anne's eyes to examine her pupils.

"Is it broken?"

"You have a severe sprain. I imagine the doctor is going to tell you to stay off your foot for a while. We extracted quite a bit of cinder and small rocks from your leg but I don't think it will scar, if that's a worry." She paused for a second then went on. "It's a good thing your husband brought you here so fast. That leg could have easily gotten infected."

"My husband?" Surely she had misunderstood.

"Your husband has been here the past three hours wearing out the floor in the waiting room. He was not a happy camper when we told him he couldn't stay in here with you. Dr. Bennett thought he was going to have a fight on his hands."

"What?" None of this made sense.

"I called the receptionist to get him when I saw you were coming around."

The door flew open and Michael rushed to the bed. Anxiety flickered across his face as he looked down at her.

"My husband?" Anne said weakly. "He's not…"

"As you can see, Mr. Brandt, your wife is fine. In a little pain, perhaps, but her ankle will be good as new in a few weeks." The nurse handed him a small bottle. "Here are some pills that will help with the pain. Make sure she takes one every four hours for the next couple of days. The doctor also recommends ice on her ankle. Just keep her off her feet for a couple of days. The doctor also wants her to wear a special medical boot that will give her a little support and stability when she tries to walk. I'll finish your paperwork so you can leave." She turned to Anne.

"You are probably going to want to sleep when you get home, Mrs. Brandt. But that's to be expected. The injection won't wear completely out for a couple of hours." With that, the nurse quickly left the room.

"Michael, damn you. How dare you tell them you're my husband." Somehow Anne's words lacked the anger she intended. She watched as a grin overtook his features. Her pulse quickened as he leaned down to kiss her forehead.

"I thought if I told them we were married, I'd have a better chance of staying with you."

Anne's heart squeezed. There was that protective thing he had going. She didn't know whether she should hug him or hit him.

"I'm taking you home," he commanded.

Before she could object, he lifted her from the bed and carried her out into the hall. He ignored the curious onlookers in the emergency area and pushed through the double doors that led to the parking lot. He carefully placed Anne inside his truck as if she were a priceless vase he didn't want to break. He rushed back to get the paperwork and boot, then slipped back into the truck and started the engine.

"Let me take care of you, Anne."

"I can take care of myself. Besides Daisy is…"

"Daisy is probably in Illinois by now. Her vacation. Remember?"

She was too tired to protest. All she wanted to do was sleep.

Once they reached the house, Michael scooped Anne in his arms and carried her inside.

"Where is your bedroom? Upstairs?"

"What?!"

"Anne, you've really got to do something about that dirty mind."

Her bedroom was large and filled with antique furniture. An oak bed with a carved headboard that nearly reached the ceiling was located in the center of the room, with a matching oak dresser gracing one wall. An ivory velvet loveseat was positioned before a bay window. He lowered her to the love seat, lifted her injured foot, and gently placed it on a soft, overstuffed ottoman nearby.

He went to the kitchen downstairs and returned with a bag filled with ice, a towel, and two bottles of water from the refrigerator. He pulled the bottle of pain pills from his pocket and put it on her night stand.

Anne watched him as he sat on the ottoman, wrapping a towel around the bag of ice before molding it around her ankle. His fingers lightly slid up her leg as he examined the ugly, multicolored bruises that had formed. His touch sent a wave of unbearable heat through her.

"Michael, thank you for bringing me home." She cleared her throat, then said, "You really don't have to stay any longer. I can take care of myself."

"I'm not leaving. Deal with it." He moved next to her on the loveseat and pulled her into his arms. He gently pressed her head against his hard chest.

All thoughts of his leaving left her as she lay against him. She closed her eyes and felt the warmth of his body, his steady heartbeat lulling her to sleep.

The morning sun blazed through the slats of the windows, bathing her bedroom in light. There were sounds from the floor below. The savory smell of bacon and toast assailed her senses and alerted her to a hunger that grew from the pit of her stomach. She brushed her hair out of her eyes, yawned then stretched. It was the piercing pain shooting up from her ankle that snapped her into reality.

When she lifted herself up to sit, the blanket slipped from her body and she realized she was in her bed—naked. Where were her clothes?! She looked around the room and spotted them neatly folded on her dresser.

"Harley, back off. That's Anne's breakfast. You already had yours." Anne jerked at the sound of Michael's voice and pulled the blanket up to cover herself. She heard him moving around in the kitchen, and then heard his footsteps on the stairs.

He appeared in the doorway with a tray of orange juice, toast, bacon and eggs, and a cup of steamy coffee. He was dressed as he had been the day before, in the gray sweatshirt and shorts.

"Michael," she began as he slid the tray on the table next to her bed. "How exactly did I fall asleep on the loveseat, yet wake up in my bed?"

"I put you there last night." He said nonchalantly, lifting the blanket at the end of the bed as he spoke.

"What are you doing?!" Anne shrieked in alarm as she held the blanket up to her neck.

"Just checking your foot." He calmly uncovered the limb in question. "It's pretty discolored and swollen this morning. Be prepared for a shock."

She peered down at her foot. It was at least twice its size and had turned multiple shades of purple during the night. The sight only momentarily distracted her from the subject at hand.

"Michael, how did my clothes get over there on my dresser?" Her face blushed vibrant shades of pink.

"I put them there after I took them off of you last night. I couldn't let you sleep in those torn and dirty clothes. I would have given you a bath but I didn't want to wake you. We can do that after breakfast."

There was a wicked glint in his eyes; a hint of a smile teased the corners of his otherwise serious face as he noted her shocked expression.

"Don't worry. I didn't look. Because if I had looked, I would have told you that you have the most amazing breasts I've ever seen." He couldn't go on. It was too damn funny. He laughed as her eyes widened.

"Exactly, where did *you* sleep last night?" Her hands formed small fists entangled in the blanket, still holding it against her neck.

"Where do you think I slept?" His gaze moved seductively to her mouth. "What are you afraid I did last night?" He moved close to her until he was sitting on the bed next to her. He slid his large hand under the blanket and across her middle until he settled on her waist. Hot flames surged through her veins at his touch.

"Michael, don't." Her heart skipped a beat; her breathing quickened.

"Are you afraid I did this?" He murmured huskily as his mouth softly moved about her face until he claimed her lips with his. The kiss was heated and demanded a response.

She dropped the blanket and weakly pushed against the granite wall of his chest. His touch ignited a fire that arose from the pit of her stomach. A fire she had never experienced before. Her pulse was racing. She felt her defenses melt away. His mouth left her lips and moved over her throat.

"Michael, stop." She sighed. The way she said his name made him more intent on his mission.

She moaned as his hand caressed her swelling breast and his lips searched for its ripe peak. When he returned to her mouth, she met him halfway with lips parted. She pulled him closer, not satisfied until she was pressing her soft body to his hard length.

She stroked the soft, fine hair that coated his muscular thigh. She wanted him. She arched up against him. She wanted him *now.*

Michael slowly pulled away. His heart beating wildly, he sat up drawing, her against his chest, stroking her hair as he cradled her head against his shoulder.

"No, honey, not like this. There are too many unanswered questions between us. I won't make love to you until you stop running from me." His voice was tender and loving. "By the way, I slept downstairs on the sofa last night, and I don't recommend it for comfort."

Hot flashes of shame scorched her face as she snatched the blanket from under him and pulled it up to her throat.

"When we make love, it will be the slow, hot, steamy kind of lovemaking that can go on for days."

"Please leave." Ice dripped from her voice. When he didn't move, she shouted, "Leave!" It was humiliating how eager she'd been to make love with him. *She* should have been the one putting on the brakes. She stiffened and pushed him away.

Anger darkened his features as he rose from the bed and stood over her. "Sometime very soon we need to talk about why you're afraid of me. Or is it that you are afraid of your feelings about me?"

He turned and strode from the room, taking the stairs two steps at a time. She heard the front door slam with a bang behind him.

Tears filled her eyes and streamed down her cheeks and throat. He was right. The feelings he evoked in her were terrifying. The body wants what the body wants. Maybe she should indulge in a fling as her friends advised. That might get him out of her system. But would it? The gamut of emotions and need he was capable of eliciting from her was something she'd never experienced. Would making love with Michael get him out of her system? Damn it, anyway. Why couldn't she be attracted to someone else—anyone else?

It was a restless night filled with boredom. She couldn't focus. Days alone with your foot propped and iced will do that to you.

She'd pick up a magazine, stare at it for a minute, and then toss it aside. There was nothing on TV even remotely interesting. Even Harley seemed bored, lying with his head resting on his long legs at her feet, his dark eyes glued on her. She needed to do something. Anything.

"Harley, let's go outside." She made her way to the front of the house and planted herself on the porch swing. The cool autumn breeze caressed her as she slowly swung back and forth. Harley sat alert sniffing the evening air, then slid down until his tummy touched the coolness of the porch floor.

She heard a noise then noticed a truck's headlights as it turned into her driveway in the distance. Harley leaped to his feet. It was a little late for company.

Harley barked then raced to the driveway. She heard a muffled voice and happy, playful sounds from her dog. The truck door slammed and a few seconds later Michael climbed the steps of the porch, Harley in tow. She hadn't seen him for three days, not that she was counting.

How he looked tonight was likely to be imprinted in her memory for a long time. He wore a tight black T-shirt that stretched across his powerful chest, and a pair of faded jeans molded to his body in all the right places. He's what her girlfriends would call "hot," but at that moment, the word didn't really do him justice.

He flashed one of his killer smiles and joined her on the swing. "Nice night, isn't it?"

"Yes." She cleared her throat. Must he sit so close?

"How's your ankle?"

"It's better."

"How much better? Still taking the pain pills?" Michael asked.

"No, not that it is any of your business."

"Just asking. The boot looks good." Actually the black and bulky medical boot looked anything but good. But it seemed to him everything about her looked good tonight—really good. She couldn't have been sexier in the plum v-neck silk sweater if she tried—boot or no boot. And knowing what he was starting to know about Anne, she didn't try. She seemed unaware of the effect she had on men in general, and on him specifically.

"Thank you." Anne said, her voice dripping with sarcasm. Amusement flickered in the eyes that met hers.

"Still afraid of me?"

"Who said I was afraid of you? That's ridiculous."

"Okay, since it's ridiculous that you might be afraid to spend some time with me, we're going for a drive. There's something I want to show you." With that, he stretched a strong hand to her, supporting her until she gained her balance then walked with her as she hobbled across the porch. He pulled open the front door and put a disappointed Harley inside the house.

This may be the worst idea ever. But she was going to show him once and for all that he had no impact on her one way or another. Was she afraid to be near him? Not.

Michael's truck rolled into the night, riding the pavement slow and easy. Windows down, the wind whipping at their clothes and hair, and Blake Shelton singing on the radio, Anne felt herself relax a little, despite herself.

When he turned onto a gravel road, the dust boiled beneath the back wheels. It wasn't long before he turned onto a dirt road that climbed a hill. Finally, he stopped. Anne watched him as he pulled the keys from the ignition and retrieved a blanket from behind the seat. He walked to the back and spread it on the truck bed.

"If you think you're getting lucky tonight, it's not happening." Anne said as he opened the passenger side door.

He smiled, ignored her remark and her protests as he pulled her out of the car and threw her over his shoulder, fireman-style.

"When was the last time you saw the Milky Way or the Big Dipper?" He set her down on the blanket in the truck bed and opened a large cooler. A breeze rustled through the trees. There was a pressure in his chest and her scent was driving him crazy. He finally nailed it. It was roses, sweet and seductive, combined with red-hot female.

"Tonight I'm serving cold beer or wine cooler. What's your pleasure?" He held a cold, dripping sample of each. She reached for the wine. They lifted their drinks, the cold liquid flowing down their throats until it warmed in the pit of their stomachs.

"I used to come here when I was in high school just to think, or when I was pissed at my parents for one thing or another. I still think it's the best spot in town." He lay back with one arm behind his head. "I've always thought the stars were magical things. There's the Big Dipper. See it?"

Anne lay back, her eyes searching the dark sky glittering with diamonds in the distance. Clouds were pressing in, but their section of sky was clear and wondrous. "Why are we here?"

"I thought it was time I introduced you to one of my favorite things—star gazing."

"Star gazing? Really? Okay, I'm curious. What are some of your other favorite things? Book clubs? Bird watching? Basket weaving? Scrapbooking?" Maybe if she said something annoying, she could focus on something besides the way his tanned skin glistened in the moonlight; the way his low voice, deep and sensual, sent a ripple through her body.

"I'm sure those are fine favorite things for some. For me, there's nothing like a cold, cold beer on a hot summer night, and slow dancing in the dark with someone that sends electricity through your body like a hot, sizzling strike of lightning. And then there's kissing." He turned on his side, his fingers intimately trailing down her cheek before he rubbed his thumb across her lower lip until he felt her tremble. "Not much can beat an evening filled with deep, hot kisses." He lay on his back gazing at the stars. "Do you agree?"

Taking a ragged breath, Anne nodded. She was speechless. Who talks like that? Something heated inside her and she wasn't thinking as clearly as she liked. His nearness, yet not touching her, was unbearable. It had been so long since she had been touched—at least not in the way Michael touched her. In her mind, she imagined the two of them, bodies melded together, dancing in the dark, swaying to the music—swaying and kissing. She wanted him, damn it. It made no sense whatsoever, but she wanted him. Anne couldn't remember ever wanting a man like she wanted him. She wanted to taste every inch of him, from his hard chest, down to his toes. Propped up on her elbow, she gazed down at him.

"What's the matter, Anne? Do I still scare you?"

That was a hot button and they both knew it. She pushed her

long hair behind her ear and slowly slid her finger up his chest to his mouth. Her long fingernails played with his lips then circled to the back of his neck as she pulled him to her. She wanted a reaction. She'd show him how unafraid of him she really was. Softly she nibbled his lower lip, and then fully pressed her lips to his. Michael's lips were hot and wet. The kind of lips one could get lost in. She pulled away and looked at him.

"Is that the best you can do?" He glanced at her with cool amusement.

Her pride seriously bruised, she felt a shudder of angry humiliation. Damn him. She pulled him closer, so close that her breasts strained against his chest. Snaking her arm around his neck, her hands now playing in his hair, her lips touching, teasing, then plunging as she poured herself into the kiss.

The sensation sent the pit of her stomach into a wild fiery swirl of need. She nibbled at his lips, teased him, and then explored the recesses of his mouth with her tongue. Exploring. Needing. Wanting. She pushed doubts or anything else out of her mind. All she could think about was him, his mouth, his strong arms tightly wound around her waist, his hard length now pressed against her until the blood pounded in her head like thunder.

Michael had imagined kissing her many, many times. But the fantasy didn't even come close. This was a million times better. He'd imagined what it would be like to feel her lips on his, her body pressed against him, but didn't bargain for the electric response surging through his body. Pressing his hand against the small of her back, he wanted to feel every cell of her being, electric current surging from her to him, a burning need demanding to be fulfilled.

Slowly Michael lifted his head and loosened his arms around her waist. He looked deeply into her eyes that fluttered open, now a swirling storm of blue. He wanted to see. No, he *needed* to see if she felt it, too. His smile was one of deep satisfaction as he watched her trembling lips, her struggle to breathe. He felt her heart racing against his chest.

"That was a m-mistake," she stuttered.

"Honey, I've made a lot of mistakes, so I know one when I see it. What just happened between the two of us was no mistake."

"Michael..." She began but stopped. What was that noise?

He heard it, too, and straightened. Thunder in the distance, and this time it wasn't her heart. "There's a storm moving in. Let's go."

Rain peppered the windshield as they made their way to Golden Acres. They were quiet, each lost in his or her own thoughts.

She needed to think long and hard about what just happened. Her body and heart had betrayed her.

He wanted to hold her hand, but knew if he reached out, she would snatch it away. He looked at her and realized by the expression on her face that her mood was darkening.

They were at her front door when he broke the silence, "So what are your favorite things?" He lazily leaned against the door frame as she reached for the door knob.

Surprised, she jerked her gaze toward him and thought carefully before she spoke. She turned, tilting her head to meet his dark eyes. Her long fingers spread and pressed against his chest. She moved closer, so close she could feel the warmth of his breath.

"I like reading a good book on a rainy day in front of a warm, crackling fire in my fireplace. There is little more satisfying than a turtle ice cream sundae when I'm feeling down, or sitting on a porch swing watching the sun set." She leaned into him, her lips inches from his, her voice husky, and whispered, "But there is nothing that comes close to dancing in the dark and sharing long, hot kisses with a man that sends heat waves through my body from my head to my toes. There is nothing to compare with making love for days with a man that is NOT my ex-husband's attorney."

Before she could weaken her control, she slipped inside and closed the door in his face.

Chapter 4

Anne gave Daisy a hug then led Harley out the back door on his leash and spotted Hank tossing a duffle bag in the back of his truck.

"Hi, Hank. Where are you headed?"

"Going to Benton County to visit some of the wind farms there." He bent down to pet Harley's head.

"Good idea. The more we learn about wind farming, the more likely we'll be successful. Dan Wright called yesterday. The deliveries of the wind turbine parts will arrive soon. He says the thing is so large, they have to deliver it in parts then put them together onsite."

"That's what I hear." He started the truck and headed toward the road.

Anne and Harley headed by foot in the same direction. Thank goodness, Hank had warmed up to the wind farm idea. His help with the project was critical.

It was early October, so the corn was almost at its tallest. Stalks as high as eleven to twelve feet cradled one to two ears of yellow corn, each protected by silk-like threads and encased in its own husk. Anne with Harley at her side briskly walked the gravel road at a clip. It was early morning and the sky was blue dotted with fluffy white clouds. The country road was deserted, save for an occasional tractor or truck.

Her ankle had healed and the exercise she craved was hers for the taking. Harley proved to be an enthusiastic partner. Autumn was Anne's favorite time of year. She loved the bright yellow, gold and red leaves that dressed the trees along the road. She had a plastic bag in her back pocket to take some leaves home to decorate the long dining room table.

It was the birds she noticed first. There were large, dark birds flying in lazy circles up ahead. Vultures. Nature's garbage disposals.

As they walked further, she noticed the stench. It assailed her senses; it was permeating and nauseating. She had never smelled anything like it. She pulled at Harley's leash to turn him around to head back to the house, but he bucked, throwing his weight into it, and yanked his leash from her hand. He began to run. Harley was running toward the area in the cornfield where the birds hovered overhead.

"Harley! Come back!" She yelled and began chasing after him. In the distance, the Schnauzer turned into the field, darting down a row of corn. Though she ran as fast as her legs could carry her, Anne didn't reach the area in time to see which row he took. "Harley! Where are you?!" Damn it. People got lost in cornfields all the time. That was the last thing she needed. She could hear the gossip about the new female farm owner who got lost in her own cornfield.

She turned into the field, unaware of the silver truck traveling toward her, the tires spinning large clouds of dust. She moved deeper within the field and the truck stopped, screeching the brakes and spitting gravel.

"Anne!" She was too far away to hear him now.

"Harley!" She screamed his name until her voice became hoarse. She couldn't go back without him and she couldn't bear it if anything happened to him. He was more than a dog, he was family.

The sickening stench was overpowering now, and her stomach was churning. She lifted her shirt to cover her nose and mouth. She kept walking, the long leaves of the stalks of corn whipping and scratching at her arms. Where was Harley?

The vultures seemed closer. She could hear them now, squawking back and forth as if in an argument. There was another sound; the buzzing of insects that grew louder as she approached.

"Harley!" She called as she crossed over several rows, still moving toward the sound of birds and insects. Soon she saw Harley's dark body about fifty feet ahead of her. She began running again, cursing the dog for not coming to her when she called.

Soon she saw thick clouds of flies. They were everywhere. She frantically swatted at them as they flew into her eyes and mouth. The pungent scent was worse the closer she got. She could barely breathe. She reached Harley and grabbed his leash before he could escape her grasp. He didn't seem to notice her. He tried to pull away. He was focused on something on the ground.

She pushed him aside and saw the maggots. It seemed like there were millions of them. "Oh, God!" she cried. It was a body. It was a woman whose face and body was covered with filth, flies and maggots. A stained blue satin ribbon was wrapped around her body with a large grotesque bow planted between her small breasts.

Anne's throat filled with bile. She fell to her knees and threw up what was left of her breakfast. She yanked on Harley's leash until he yelped to get him to move. She stumbled and pulled Harley in the direction she prayed was the road. She patted her pocket for her cell phone. It wasn't there! Shit, it was back at the house. Adrenaline kicked in and she began running, Harley at her side. Over and over, she repeated, "I can't get lost in here. I can't."

She prayed she was heading in the right direction. She had to find the road. If she got lost in this cornfield, who knows how long it would be before someone found her. She felt hot tears flowing down her cheeks and realized she was crying.

She saw something silver flickering in the distance and aimed toward it. Up closer, she saw the road and realized she was seeing a silver truck. There was a man leaning against it talking on a cell phone. Michael!

"Help!" Anne screamed. Her tears were blinding now but her legs kept moving. She flew across the road, Harley in tow, slamming against Michael, sending his cell phone flying and the three of them tumbling down a ditch.

"What the hell?!" Michael exclaimed as she clung to him, her nails digging into his back. She was crying hysterically and he couldn't understand what she was saying. Harley was barking and trying to pull his leash out of her hand. Michael tried to stand but, she wouldn't loosen her grip on him.

"Anne, what's going on? What's in the field? Honey, look at me!"

Her mouth moved, but nothing that came out made sense. She thought she was going to be sick again. No. Not now.

"Body." She had to make him understand. Harley continued barking and pulling at his leash.

"What?" Michael pulled Anne to her feet and moved her toward his truck. He opened the door, snapped his fingers, and Harley jumped in. He closed the door and pulled her against him, rubbing her back to calm her. "Okay, now try again. What happened?"

"There's a body in the field." There, it was out. "Harley found her."

"Shit. Stay here. Don't move." He gently pushed her against the truck, stepped back to make sure her legs would hold, then ran toward the ditch. "I've got to find my cell phone."

Moments later she could hear him talking. He seemed to be giving orders to someone. Finally, he came around the truck growling at someone on the phone. "Get out here NOW! Send the crime techs and the M.E., too. A body was just found on Corey Road on Golden Acres Farm. Look for my truck."

Michael threw his cell on the dash and pulled Anne into his arms, holding her as tightly as he could, his heart beating as erratically as hers.

Once her initial shock had worn off, she shivered, though she wasn't cold. There was a dead woman in her cornfield. *Her* cornfield. Just thinking of it shattered her. Someone's mother, sister or daughter lay dead in her field to rot like garbage. Who could have done this? Who ended this woman's life and chose to dump her body in Anne's field? It wasn't like her farm was close to a heavily travelled road like an interstate. How did the killer know the location of her farm? Icy fear twisted around her heart and clamped tight.

Once they secured the area with crime scene tape, deputies moved in and out of the field, sometimes stopping to talk to each other. Michael stood near his truck, having an apparently serious conversation with Sheriff David E. Miller, who appeared to be a jerk of epic proportion. As soon as Miller discovered she'd found the body, he sequestered Anne to the back seat of his car until he had a chance to talk to her further. What was there to talk about?

A news truck pulled up, and a woman in a suit holding a microphone hurried past, along with a cameraman. They were stopped by a deputy, who was then peppered with questions.

The longer Anne sat in the back of the sheriff's car, the more pissed she became. Why couldn't she be standing out there with the rest of them? Why couldn't she have stayed in Michael's truck? Better yet, why couldn't she and Harley go home? They both smelled like rotting garbage. The stench coated every inch of her body and hair like a stinking, sticky film. Enough was enough.

She flew out of the back seat, slamming the door behind her. She wasn't a freaking criminal. She was sick of waiting, tired of being ignored. She was going home, damn it.

The sheriff was the first to bear the brunt of her wrath. She tapped his shoulder and said. "Excuse me, my name is Anne Mason. You might remember me. I'm the one who's been stuck in the back of your freaking car for what seems like hours. Unless I'm a suspect and you're going to arrest me, I'm going home."

Her tone angered him. Who the hell did this woman think she was, challenging his authority like that in front of his deputies? "If I tell you to stay in the back of my car, then you damn well better stay there until I get around to you."

She opened her mouth to give a stinging retort when she noticed a petite woman racing toward them with a white envelope that she shoved in Michael's hand.

He opened the envelope, reviewed its contents, and handed it to the sheriff. "This is the search warrant we need. Send the crime scene team in to process the area."

Anne glared at the sheriff with burning, reproachful eyes, and turned to Michael, who had not missed her flare of temper. "May I borrow your cell phone? I need to make a call to my attorney."

"Not necessary. I'll take you home."

His dark eyes focused on the sheriff. "She found the body. It's unlikely she dumped it in her own field. If you have any questions, you can find her at her house down the road. You know where it is."

The sheriff walked away muttering something under his breath as Michael opened the passenger side of his truck. Anne pushed Harley aside and got in. Michael jumped in the truck and turned his key in the ignition.

He glanced at Anne, her face filled with fear and anger. He wanted to distract her from the horror she had just seen.

"You two have got to do something about that smell. You're ripe." He rolled all the windows down and switched the air conditioner to high.

"If that was humor, Michael, please notice I'm not laughing." She glared at him as he regarded her with amusement. She was definitely distracted. She made a low, tired sigh. "Would you please step on the gas? I desperately need an hour, maybe two in a hot shower. Hopefully, I'll be able to scrub this unholy stench from my body."

He was grateful she seemed calmer now, color returning to her face. She was terrified when she slammed into him, and that fear pissed him off. If the sick fuck who put the body in her field thought he was going to mess with her further, he better think again. And that cocky sheriff had better get his ass in gear, because he needed to find the sicko sooner rather than later, or he'd be looking for another job.

Michael turned into her driveway looking sidelong at the dog. "Harley, you better prepare yourself for a long, hot bath, and a little of Daisy's temper when she smells your stinky self."

The moment the truck stopped, Anne flew into the house, climbing the stairs two at a time, stripping off her clothes as she went. Michael waited for Harley to jump down, then led him to the back of the house in search of Daisy.

After he helped Daisy drag a child's swimming pool to the patio, Michael headed for the house, as water and dog splashed behind him. He heard a couple of swear words he didn't know were in Daisy's vocabulary, and bee-lined for the safety of Anne's house.

By the time he reached the stairs, he heard the shower running. He slowly climbed every step, noting each discarded garment as he went. He liked the pink lace bra and panties, and thought how much he would have liked to be the one removing them. Damn. Couldn't he get her out of his head for a minute?! He should be back at the crime scene.

In her room, Michael sat on the loveseat and listened to Anne in the shower, trying not to imagine what it would be like to join her, washing every inch of her curves with frothy suds. He'd imagined her naked a lot lately, and had the urge to remove his clothes and join her there. The sweet scent of roses wafted through the room. He could drown in that scent.

Anne scrubbed herself head to toe four times and prayed that was enough to get rid of the stench. She washed and rinsed her hair again and again. Finally, she slipped out of the shower, rubbed some baby oil into her skin, and dotted off the moisture with a soft towel. She tossed the towel wrapped around her in the hamper then stepped into the bedroom to her mirrored dresser to find something to wear.

He watched her in awe. She was like a tall, ice-cold glass of wine in the hottest of summer days. One sip was not going to be enough. Not even close.

"Looks like you may have removed the first layer of skin." His voice was low and husky. Looking at her skin all pink and glistening, it was a wonder he could speak at all.

She whirled around, spotting him on her loveseat. "What the hell are you doing in my bedroom *again*?! Get out!"

His gaze dropped appreciably from her eyes to her toes. "I can't stay long."

"I hope I can hide my disappointment." She rushed to the bathroom for a towel, which she whipped around her body.

"I wanted to make sure you were okay before I go."

"I'm fine. Thanks for the ride, Michael. The peep show is on the house. Now leave."

"I'll call you later." He closed the door slowly, with a grin that quickly spread across his face.

There was a sparkle in Daisy's eyes and one eyebrow raised when she met him on the stairs. The lacy bra and panties dangled from one finger. They talked a moment before he bounded down the stairs and out the door.

Anne was pulling clothes from the drawers when she heard a knock on the door. "Michael, that better not be you." She growled through her teeth.

The door opened and Daisy peered inside. "Oh, Daisy, I'm sorry. I thought…"

"No worries. I wanted to check on you once I got Harley cleaned up. Are you okay?" Concern swept across Daisy's face.

"Yes." Lie. She was anything but.

"What a horrible thing to happen, you finding that body. It makes me sick to think about it."

"I know the feeling." Her stomach was still in a sickening spin.

"Michael told me to tell you that he had to get back to the crime scene. He gave me his cell phone number in case you need anything." She paused. "That man jumped headfirst into the fire, didn't he?"

"What do you mean?"

"He hasn't even been officially on the job for a week."

"What are you talking about, Daisy?"

"I thought you knew. Michael Brandt is the new county prosecutor. This is his first case and may turn out to be the biggest thing that's hit our area for a hundred years."

They were loading the body into the ambulance when Michael returned. He saw a crime scene tech and pulled her aside. "What do you have?"

"It's a woman, a young one. She's probably in her early twenties."

"You don't think it's…"

"I hope not, but it looks like it might be the Mitchell girl who disappeared a while back."

"The one who went missing from college?"

"Yes. Definitely a homicide. We'll find out more at the autopsy. There is something else. It's odd about the way we found her."

"What do you mean?"

"There is a blue ribbon wound around her body several times. It's attached to a large blue bow, the kind you'd find on a big gift box."

"Christ. What's that all about?"

"I just talked to the coroner, Doc Meade. He's coming in. He says he will work all night if he needs to, to complete the autopsy."

He watched her head toward the coroners' van, jumping in the back as another crime scene tech held the door. "Tell Doc Meade I want the autopsy report as soon as he can get it to me." He slammed the door and the vehicle headed toward town. He saw the sheriff and moved to join him.

"Did your deputies find anything near the body?"

"Nope. They're taking a short break, and then they're going to search the field again along with the Crime Scene Techs."

"What are they talking about?" Michael asked the sheriff as he watched three deputies huddled nearby.

"They are probably betting on who gets to watch the hot redhead that was in the back of my car if someone decides she needs protection."

"Sounds like you've got quite a team. Do they always think with their dicks instead of their brains? You can tell them for me that if they don't put their full attention on this case, they'll be looking for a new line of work." He ground the words out between his teeth.

When he turned to meet his hostile glare, the sheriff realized Michael was deadly serious, and headed out to talk to his deputies.

By the time he got back to Anne's house, the late afternoon sun was setting. Michael was dead-tired, and the last place he should be was Anne's home. It was an active investigation now. She'd have questions, and as a prosecutor, he couldn't answer them. But his protective streak had returned full throttle, and all he could think about was the pure terror in her eyes when she slammed into him. The body being dumped in her field could have been a random act, but what if it wasn't? He eased out of the truck and pulled a large brown bag from the passenger seat, then strode toward the house.

With a soft, small blanket wrapped around her shoulders, Anne sat on the porch swing, sipping a glass of wine. A half-empty bottle and a couple of glasses lay on the table beside her. Her face was pale, her expression apprehensive and he didn't have to guess what she was thinking about.

He eased into a wicker chair near her, placing the brown bag at his feet.

"What's in the bag?"

"I hope you're hungry. I haven't eaten all day and I'm starving. I picked up some sandwiches, slaw and fries from the barbecue place in town."

"I can't even think about food. I wonder if I will ever get that body out of my head—or the smell out of my nose." A wave of queasiness moved through her.

"So how much wine have you had on an empty stomach?" He poured a glass for himself and rummaged through the food bag. He slipped a couple of fries in his mouth as he searched for the sandwiches.

"Not enough. So don't even think about taking advantage of me." She watched him unwrap a barbeque sandwich then devour it. He offered her some fries but she shook her head.

"I was worried about you taking advantage of *me*." His mischievous grin made her laugh in spite of herself. "I haven't forgotten how you tried to have your way with me in the back of my truck." A vaguely sensuous light passed between them.

Changing the subject before her mind could wander in a dangerous direction, she said, "Why didn't you tell me you're the new county prosecutor?'

"It was in the papers, I thought you knew."

She shook her head and asked, "Have they identified her?"

"Who?"

"The dead woman in my field."

"No, not yet."

"Is she the missing Mitchell girl?"

He scanned her face and decided not to tell her that he thought the body was the missing college girl. She'd been through enough today and still had the night ahead of her. He'd wait until they made a definite identification.

"Don't know."

"How could anyone hurt her like that and just dump her like she was a bag of trash, out in the open where animals and insects can get to her? Who *does* that?"

"We may never have the answer to that question."

She needed a distraction. She had thought of nothing but the body for hours, so she changed the topic. "So why did you leave your cushy law practice?"

"I'm not sure you'd understand, or believe me if I told you."

"Try me."

"I found I have a talent for convincing judges and juries the people I represent are innocent, whether they are or not."

"Sounds like you developed a conscience."

"Something like that. I couldn't stop thinking of the ones I got off, who are probably out there doing more of what they got arrested for in the first place."

Anne watched him thoughtfully. This was not something she expected to hear from him, and it surprised her. She'd assumed he enjoyed his role as a defense attorney.

"It sounds like most of your cases were criminal in nature. If that's true, why did you represent Allan?"

He gazed at her, realizing this topic had been the elephant in the room for too long.

"A friend of mine convinced me to take on a divorce case. I've never liked divorce cases, but I took this one because I owed him a favor. I met with my new client a couple of times and began to feel a little sorry for the guy whose wife was cheating on him and depleting his bank account. So I decided to get the poor guy a little justice. I believed him. He had me hook, line and sinker."

"I don't want to hear this." She started to get up, but he pulled her back down.

"So I represented Allan Long and at the hearing I realized he'd given me nothing but bad information—about his finances and you. In addition, he conveniently didn't tell me his gambling problem had depleted his banking accounts, not his wife. By the time I realized he'd lied to me, it's too late."

"Do you still represent him?"

"I dropped Allan as a client within five minutes of the end of the hearing. I don't like to be lied to. He's lucky we were in the judge's chambers, or I might have kicked his lying ass."

Anne stared at Michael, not knowing what to say, or how to respond. How could she blame him for believing Allan, when she'd done the same thing for years?

Harley bounded onto the porch with a ball in his mouth, as Daisy joined them. Soon Michael was in the yard, throwing the ball, and a delighted Harley was bounding from one area of the yard to another to fetch it.

"Give him a chance, Anne." Daisy said softly as she watched Michael and the big dog interact.

"Not going to happen." Anne lifted the glass to her lips to sip the wine.

"I think he may be in love with you." Daisy stated evenly, watching Anne for a reaction.

"What?!" Anne coughed, nearly choking on the wine.

"You have feelings for him, too. I can tell by the way you look at him when you don't think anyone is looking."

"Nothing could be farther from the truth." Yes, she was attracted to the man, but that was probably just sex, something she hadn't had in a year or so.

Daisy reached over to pat Anne's hand. "I want to see you happy. You deserve so much more from a man that you ever got from your bastard ex-husband. I think Michael could make you happy."

"A lot has happened today, Daisy. Romance is the last thing on my mind right now."

"Okay, I'll leave it alone for now."

"Thank you," Anne said quietly.

Daisy placed two fingers in her mouth and whistled. "Come on, Harley, it's dinner time."

Michael joined Anne on the swing and put his arm around her shoulders. She unconsciously leaned against his hard, warm body.

"Are you going to be okay tonight? Want me to stay over? I can sleep on the sofa."

"No, thanks," she replied, a little too quickly. Michael staying over was a colossally bad idea. She wasn't sure how much longer she could keep him out of her bed. But she certainly wasn't in the mood tonight to debate the issue.

"If you're sure you don't want me to stay, come walk me to my truck." He reached out, caught her hand in his, and pulled her from the swing. He glanced at her and realized the strained, stricken look had returned to her face. It took every ounce of self-control to stop himself from throwing her over his shoulder; taking her to her bedroom, and spending the rest of the night making her forget what she had seen today.

He leaned against the truck and looked down at her.

"I think we should kiss." He spoke in a casual, mischievous way, hiding the need in his voice.

"Not a good idea." *Definitely* not a good idea. She remembered the way he made her feel in the back of his truck under the stars. The heat and need was unbearable. She had enough on her mind already.

"I think if the idea was part of a top 10 list of good ideas, it would be number one." He teased.

"Okay, one kiss." Why not? He was so persistent. He was never going to leave until she kissed him. Fingers spread across his hard chest; she stood on the tips of her toes and lightly pecked him on the cheek.

"Give me a break. If you think that was a kiss, we've got some serious practice to do." He wound his arms around her waist and gently pulled her closer. "That was *not* a kiss."

His kiss was slow and thoughtful, his tongue exploring. It left her wanting more; a surprising want and need flickered through her veins. She leaned into Michael, tightening her arms around his neck.

The kiss ended far too soon. She watched him as he got into the truck. The amused look had left his face and was replaced with a spark of indefinable emotions swirling in his eyes.

She entered the house, locked the door and headed upstairs for another shower—a cold one this time.

The house was dark as he expected. Three in the morning was an ungodly time to be up and around. This he counted on. His old Mustang coasted to a stop in front of her mailbox. With a gloved hand, he slid the envelope inside and closed the lid.

They'd found the body. A rush of exhilaration swept over him. Who knew the discovery of his handiwork would be this thrilling? They'd pay attention to him now and recognize him for the important person he was. The bastards who'd ruined his life would see he was a force to be reckoned with. Who the fuck did they think they were dealing with?

He would have loved to have seen their faces when they discovered how he'd staged the body. The ribbon wrapped around the corpse and the gift bow were genius additions. Hopefully, that bitch Anne Mason was smart enough to understand the significance. If not, she would once she read his note. Her first gift. But not the last one. There were more offerings to come.

They'd ruined his life. He'd take theirs.

Chapter 5

The night was thick with dense, impenetrable fog, and she was running in the cornfield. Long, razor-sharp leaves sliced at her as she ran past, making long cuts in her skin. She looked down to see streams of blood running in rivulets down her arms and legs.

She was lost. There was good chance she was running in circles and she was terrified she would never get out of the field. She wanted to scream for help, but every time she tried, her vocal chords failed her. Her heart was beating out of her chest. The simple act of breathing became more and more difficult. She began wheezing, the pressure in her chest unbearable.

She heard the muffled sound of footsteps in the thick overturned earth, whirled, and saw a dark shadow in the distance. Sensing something sinister, she pushed forward. The figure moved toward her. She ran faster and faster.

Suddenly she was falling—falling in slow motion until she hit the ground with a resounding thud. Oh, God, where was the dark figure? Was he still behind her? She rolled onto her back. It was then she realized she was not alone. Someone lay near her on the ground.

Turning her head, she strained to see in the thick darkness. A loud buzzing sound assailed her ears as hundreds of flies attacked her eyes and mouth. Her hands batted at them but they kept coming. Razor beams of moonlight cut through the fog and finally she could see a body, or what was left of it, as the maggots quenched their hunger. She was screaming now. She had found her voice.

"Noooo!" Anne gasped, panting in terror. The shriek jerked her awake and shaken. It was the third nightmare that night, identical to the two before. Harley jumped onto her bed and she screamed again.

The dog tilted his head and gazed at her with a questioning look. She patted Harley as he nudged her with his head.

She sat up to check her alarm clock. It was four in the morning. She moved to the windows across the room, opened the shutters, and sat down on the loveseat to gaze out the window. Darkness washed over her yard and the surrounding fields, but in a streak of faint light in the dark sky, she saw the promise of dawn. The house was quiet. She wrapped her arms around her legs and rested her head on her knees for a moment. She took a deep breath and willed her heartbeat to slow.

She quietly walked to her office, turned on her computer and desk lamp, then watched as the large monitor came to life. She answered a few emails, then worked on a software design for a company contracting her services. There was about a month of work left on the project before it went into user testing.

She logged onto the Internet and typed in the address for the local news website, then rose to open each of three windows in the room. No matter how brisk, she needed some air. Harley stuck his long nose out the first window and sniffed the fresh air before crossing the room and settling down near her desk chair. At the third window, she noticed the lights were on in Hank's apartment above the garage. He was back from Benton County. He must be an early riser, she thought, or maybe he had a case of insomnia too. She wondered if anyone had told him about the body.

She threw a soft, rose cashmere wrap about her shoulders and returned to the computer screen. The headline on the home page was: Woman Finds Body. She scrolled past advertisements until she reached a large color photo of herself sitting in the back of the sheriff's car. Oh, hell no. She continued to curse as she moved to the story itself.

She began reading aloud. "Anne Mason of Golden Acres Farm was walking her dog yesterday when she made a grisly discovery. She found a body decomposing in a cornfield near her house. Investigators working the case are not talking, but there are rumors the body may be that of Rachel Mitchell, a college student who has been missing since August. A full autopsy to determine identification and cause of death is pending, as is notification of next of kin." Please, God, she thought. Please don't let it be the missing student.

She heard a noise down the hall, then saw Daisy moving toward her with a large mug of steaming coffee. "It looks like someone else is having trouble sleeping."

"Daisy, come look at this story."

Daisy pulled a chair next to Anne. "Why the hell did they use your photo?! And they took it while you were in the back seat of a police car? Freaking idiots. It makes you look like a damn criminal."

"I had thoughts along the same line." She pointed to the second paragraph of the article. "But keep reading. They think the body I found yesterday might be Rachel Mitchell."

"Oh my God, it just can't be her. I just visited with her mother the other day and helped her post some missing flyers. She is hanging onto her sanity with a thin thread," said Daisy, trying to hide the quick tears that came to her eyes.

"Daisy, they don't have identification yet. It might *not* be her." Wishful thinking. She hoped it wasn't Rachel, but there was a good chance it was.

"Why did he choose to dump the body in our field?"

"I've been asking myself the same thing. It's not like our land is easy to find. Does that mean he's from this area? Does it mean he is familiar with our farm? Is it someone we know?" They were unsettling questions she couldn't stop asking herself.

"I can't believe anyone we know could do something this horrible."

"I don't want to believe it either."

They both were startled by the sound of the doorbell. "Who could that be at this hour of the morning? It's barely six." Daisy pulled her robe around her waist a little tighter, and headed downstairs to the front door. Anne heard some brief conversation, then heard Daisy coming back up the stairs.

"Anne, Sheriff Miller is here. He wants to ask you a few questions. I told him to wait in the kitchen while we got dressed."

By the time Anne reached the kitchen, the coffee was brewing, while eggs and bacon were frying in a pan. The delicious breakfast scents filled her senses as she entered the room. Her empty stomach reminded her she hadn't eaten since early yesterday, and she was starving. Sheriff Miller sat at the round oak table, absently petting Harley as he watched Daisy cook.

Anne gazed at the sheriff as she sat down. He was a tall man in his fifties, with his premature white hair in a military-style buzz cut. He sat across the table from her, his posture ramrod stiff and a frown crossed his face. Daisy had told Anne that he was a former Army MP who preferred to be called Sheriff Miller, as if "Sheriff" were his first name. Daisy thought those who called Miller by his actual first name were probably limited to his immediate family. Daisy had said she was surprised he didn't expect people to salute him—including his wife. His no-nonsense style had led the county sheriff department for almost eight years.

"Good morning, Sheriff Miller," said Anne, as Daisy brought three cups of steaming coffee to the table.

"Good morning, Ms. Mason. I'm sorry about being here so early, but we're chasing our tails at the station. The media has been driving us nuts since the body was found. I've got a couple of questions for you. I thought we could get this out of the way before I headed in to work." In actuality, he had planned to visit her at 9:00 o'clock, but when he couldn't sleep, he decided to head over. People had a way of opening up more when his visits surprised them.

Daisy brought over plates of eggs, bacon and toast, and sat down next to Anne.

"Ms. Daisy, you didn't have to go to this trouble," said Sheriff Miller, as he dived into his food.

"No trouble. We don't often have a guest for breakfast."

"What is it you want to know?" Anne was on her second cup of coffee and thankfully could feel the caffeine kicking in. The ache in her head reminded her what a hellish night she'd had. No sleep will do that to you, she thought.

"Ms. Mason, let's talk about how you happened to find the body in your field."

"Call me Anne. What would you like to know?" She smeared

butter and some strawberry jam on her toast and took a bite.

"Why don't you start from the beginning, and tell me how you knew the body would be in your field?" He said the words calmly, as if there weren't an accusation sewn in the question.

"I *didn't* know the body would be in my field. What are you getting at?"

Daisy nearly jumped out of her chair. "You've got to be kidding! You can't be suggesting Anne knew that body was there!" Daisy spat her words, so furious she couldn't get the words out fast enough. Anne placed her hand on Daisy's arm to calm her. The sheriff glared at Daisy, then looked down at his food, choosing to ignore her outburst.

"I think I'll leave you two to talk alone." With that Daisy left the room, still seriously pissed off about the sheriff's insinuation.

"Anne, just start from the beginning." His cool gaze met hers over the rim of his coffee cup.

"I was taking a walk. Harley was with me."

"Is there any reason why you chose that particular area for your walk?"

"Yes, the fall is my favorite time of year. There are more trees down that road and I wanted to see if the leaves had turned."

"Was Harley on a leash?"

"Yes."

"The location of the body was deep within your field. Tell me how you happened to find it."

"I noticed this horrible smell and there were vultures circling an area in the field. Harley must have noticed it, too, because he broke away from me. He ran into the cornfield. I ran after him. He's a house dog, and I was afraid he could get lost in the field if I didn't catch him."

"So you followed the dog into the cornfield. Didn't you worry that *you* would get lost in there? Last year we had to get out the 'copter to find a couple of tourists who got lost in a cornfield on the Francis farm. Scared them silly."

"I wasn't thinking about that. I needed to catch Harley. When I finally found him, he was standing over the body. I grabbed his leash and dragged him out of the field. I ran for a long time, looking for the road. There was a point I thought I might be lost, but eventually I saw the road and Michael Brandt's truck. I ran to him for help."

Miller chugged the last of his coffee, set the mug down, and turned to Anne. "I'll let you know if I have any additional questions. Thanks for the hospitality."

"Before you go, I have some questions," said Anne.

"Go ahead."

"Wouldn't the killer have to be a local? I mean, if you're driving here from town, you have to make at least 15 turns to get here."

"Maybe. That would take the randomness out of the equation, wouldn't it? Good point, Ms. Mason."

"Why choose my field? There are farms all over the state. Why choose Golden Acres to dump a body?

"That is a question I have, too." The suspicious look he gave her was not lost on Anne. He actually suspected she had something to do with this crime. Unbelievable.

"You're not going out of town anytime soon, are you?" He pushed his chair back, stood up, and looked down at Anne with his trademark frown.

"I don't have any trips planned."

"Good. Just want to make sure I can reach you if I have more questions." He walked to the front door, his boots making a thud on the oak plank floor with each step.

Daisy opened the back door, then placed a couple of boxes and a stack of letters on the table. She was still steaming. "Sheriff Miller has earned my nomination for asshole of the year. Whoever he's running against during re-election has my vote. Here's yesterday's mail. I walked down to the mailbox to cool off. He made me so damn mad I had to do something."

"He actually thinks I might have something to do with this."

"He's a freaking idiot."

"I'd have to be pretty stupid to kill someone then dump the body in my own field."

"No kidding." said Daisy as she rolled her eyes. "I'm going upstairs to get ready to drive into town to get our groceries."

Anne was shuffling through the mail when a letter fell to the floor. As she lifted the envelope to place it on the table, she noticed there was no return address or postage stamp. That's odd. She ran her nail under the flap and dumped its contents. Inside was a copy of the article she found on the Web on how she found the body, along with a note.

> *Anne,*
> *Nice article. Great photo.*
> *I do all the hard work and you get all the press.*
> *I'm glad you found my gift.*
> *Just a little gesture to let you know you're on my mind.*
> *Not much time left until I come for you.*

Icy fingers of fear clutched at her throat as she read, then re-read the note.

It was mid-afternoon before Michael could get Sheriff Miller and Doc Meade in his office for a preliminary report about the autopsy results, and an update from the investigative unit.

"Do you have an identification of the body?" One of Michael's chief concerns was that they wouldn't be able to identify the body.

"Yes, we did. It's Rachel Mitchell. We've had her dental records for months. We'd hoped we wouldn't need them," said Doc Meade.

"Shit."

"This is a strange one," Doc Meade began.

"Define 'strange.'" Michael's frown deepened.

"For one thing, the body was nude and had been washed down with bleach to remove forensic evidence. Most killers would not know to do unless he's watched a hell of a lot of CSI on television." the doctor said. "He went to extremes to destroy evidence that would lead us to him. My guess is that this is not the first violent crime for our killer. I'll bet he's even served time for a violent crime. He's determined not to get caught again, and has taken measures to make sure he isn't."

"Yeah, you may be right," said the sheriff.

"There's more. There are no prints on the blue ribbon he tied around the body, or on the bow. Killer used gloves. I'm no profiler, but I'm guessing that ribbon and bow represents something to the killer. Maybe something he is trying to communicate. This is pretty sick, but is he saying the dead body is a gift or something? And who is he trying to communicate with?"

"It's not an M.O. I've ever heard of." Michael turned to the sheriff. "Check the database to see if it's been used before."

Sheriff Miller nodded, then asked, "What about sexual assault?"

"No vaginal trauma. So no."

"Cause of death?" Michael leaned forward putting his elbows on his desk, his head in his hands.

"Definitely homicide. More specifically strangulation. The hyoid bone in her neck was broken. He strangled her with his hands. Also, there were small burns about 3.5 centimeters apart on her neck and back, matching the prongs of a stun gun, so that is how he controlled her."

"Time of death?" Sheriff Miller asked as he jotted notes in his tablet.

"Judging from the level of decomp and the maggots, my guess is anywhere from four to seven days. If you need a timeline more definite than that, we're going to have to contact a bug guy."

"Four to seven days? But Rachel Mitchell disappeared on August 30th. So the bastard held her at another location? For almost a month and a half? What the hell are we dealing with?" Agitated, the sheriff rose from his chair and went to the large window that faced the street. His brows drew together in an angry scowl.

"What about your team, sheriff? Did they find anything?" asked Michael.

"Not much. Thanks to the hard rain we had last week, there were no footprints, except for those belonging to Anne Mason and her dog. No tire tracks either."

Michael's secretary opened the office door to announce he had another meeting in five minutes.

Michael nodded, then turned to the two men.

"I want this case to be your first priority. Another thing, no information from the crime scene or autopsy gets to the media. Is that understood?"

The sheriff retrieved his hat and sadly placed it on his head. "I'll go to the Mitchells now. It's time they knew their daughter isn't coming home."

Something had happened. Whatever it was, it wasn't good. Michael could see it in her eyes, even from a distance, as the restaurant hostess led him to the table where she sat.

Anne was sitting next to a huge stone fireplace, her eyes dark as she watched him approach the table. Her smile was brief and unnatural. There was a half-empty wine bottle on the table. Something was definitely up.

"I was surprised to get your message." His gaze searched her face as he sat down.

"Your secretary said your schedule was booked, but I thought you must take time to eat." She was using all of the self-discipline she had to stay calm. This was no time to freak out. Yes, she needed to hand over the note, but she needed information, too. If she didn't play this right, she wouldn't get it.

"Yes, dinner is definitely a good idea. I'm starved." Something's up. He'd asked her to dinner a half-dozen times and she'd said no each time. Now she calls him out of the blue and wants him to meet her here.

"I heard you got the autopsy results today and that the body in my field is Rachel Mitchell." Lie. No one had told her a thing about the case.

"News travels fast around here. Yes, it was Rachel."

"Her poor family. I can't imagine the kind of pain they must be in now."

He nodded in agreement. He got the waitress's attention and ordered a bottle of Coors. He gazed at Anne, who was shifting in her seat, looking uncomfortable.

"Why do you think her body was left in my field?"

"It was probably accidental. The killer may have been driving around looking for a place to dump her and by sheer luck came upon your field."

"Did you know that if you were driving from town you would have to make fifteen turns to arrive at that particular cornfield?"

"No." His eyebrows rose questioningly.

"It *wasn't* an accident the body was dumped at Golden Acres." She slid a plastic bag across the table toward him and watched his face as he reviewed the article, then the note.

Anne,
Nice article. Nice photo.
I do all the hard work and you get all the press.
I'm glad you found my gift.
Just a little gesture to let you know you're on my mind.
Not much time left until I come for you.

Gift? His mind went back to the meeting when Doc Meade described the blue bow and ribbon that was tied around the body. The killer was trying to communicate something. To Anne? Christ, he's targeting Anne. He gritted his teeth as he stared at the note. The idea of someone doing to Anne what was done to Rachel Mitchell made his blood boil. Not going to happen.

"How did you get this?"

"It was left in our mailbox with the rest of the mail this morning. It's not a prank, is it?"

"No, I don't think it's a prank. We've got to get this to the sheriff. There might be a fingerprint, DNA, or something on it." He pulled a pen out of his jacket pocket and used it to carefully push the folded paper back into the plastic Ziploc bag. He pulled out his cell phone and punched in some numbers.

"Excuse me for a minute. I need to talk to the sheriff. Don't go anywhere. I'll be right back." Gripping his cell phone to his ear, he raced out the restaurant to the sidewalk. Anne watched Michael through the front window, pacing as he talked. He soon returned to the table.

"Michael, I need to know everything you know about Rachel's murder."

"Anne, I can't comment about an ongoing investigation."

"Bullshit. He's targeting me. I need to know what you know." She glared at him, her anger threatening to boil over. The couple in the table next to them curiously glanced at her, and then went back to their meal.

"I can't talk to you or anyone else about an ongoing

investigation." With the addition of the note to the investigation, she was now more than a witness who found the body. She played an integral role in the investigation. Any information flow from this point forward had to be one-way, and from her. Shit. Talk about a complication. A prosecutor can't have a relationship with someone this close to a case. Not if he didn't want to get slapped with a conflict-of-interest accusation.

She looked up to see Sheriff Miller moving toward their table. He nodded to her, shook hands with Michael, and sat down.

"Where's the note?" He looked at Anne with an expression she couldn't read, and then turned to Michael, who shoved the note in the plastic bag toward him.

"So you got this note after I left your house this morning?"

"Yes, it was in a stack of mail that Daisy brought in," said Anne.

He didn't say anything. He just stared at her.

"What?"

"Nothing. I'll get this to our crime techs." He put the note in his pocket, then continued. "Do you mind if I ask you a few questions?"

"What do you want to know?" With an eyebrow raised she gazed at him.

"Have you had any trouble lately? Anything at work?"

"No. My partner at the computer company, Richard Thompson, was disappointed that I was leaving, but there was no anger or anything."

"Have you noticed anything odd like someone following you? Any hang-up calls?" He pulled out a small pad from his jacket and started taking notes.

"I was carjacked a couple of months ago. He was never caught."

"Where did this happen?"

"In Indianapolis."

"How about your personal life? Is anyone angry with you?"

"Besides my ex-husband, no." What personal life? Not that it was any of his business, but she hadn't had one in a long time. She'd worked long hours, and she and Allan avoided each other the last year of their marriage.

"What about your ex-husband? Is he angry enough to try to hurt you?"

"If you are asking me if he would murder a college student and dump her body in my field, the answer is no. Allan's a jerk but he's not a killer."

"I'm having him checked out anyway."

"It's not Allan."

"We'll see."

"Can you tell me if you have any suspects for Rachel's murder?" Anne looked at him long and hard. It was his turn for questions.

"No suspects right now. We're going to re-interview anyone we talked to when we first discovered Rachel was missing. See if anything shakes out. But for now, I'm going to get this note to our lab. If you think of anything else, call me."

Anne watched the sheriff as he strode toward the door. She wasn't at all sure he believed anything she told him. Did he really suspect her, or was it his job to suspect everyone and everything? At any rate, she didn't like him.

The waitress brought a bottle of Coors and placed it before Michael. She asked if they were ready to order and he ordered some appetizers. The way Anne was downing the wine; he needed to get something in her stomach.

"You might want to slow down on the wine." He reached for her hand and squeezed it.

She snatched her hand back and said, "Easy for you to say. You're not wearing a psycho-killer's target on your back."

"Anne, I'll talk to the sheriff to see if he can get a deputy to watch your house. In the meantime, I want you to consider adding more security. Your front door doesn't even have a deadbolt."

"Marion never saw a need…"

"*You* have a need. Check the windows and doors for the condition of all your locks today."

"Okay, that's probably a good idea."

"Do you want me to follow you home?"

"No, that's not necessary. I'm fully capable of getting myself home safely."

"I think I should stay over tonight."

"No. I shouldn't have told you about the note."

"Why not?"

"Because now you're in major guard dog mode. I don't need a man to rescue me. I'm not one of those dependent, helpless women who can't even make a decision about her own safety." She glared at Michael, grabbed her purse and jumped to her feet. She ignored his angry stare that was burning a hole in her back as she left the restaurant.

Chapter 6

Someone was pounding something somewhere and pain throbbed through her head with each pound. The sound grew louder until it jerked her awake. She looked at the alarm clock on her bedside table. Damn it. It was one in the morning. And someone was beating on her front door. A sliver of fear sliced through her as she opened a drawer and took out her Glock 21. She crept down the stairs. The pounding continued. She moved two feet before the door and lifted her gun ready to shoot.

"Who's there?"

"Michael. Let me in."

Damn him. She whipped the door open. "What in the hell are you doing? You almost gave me a cardiac arrest. Do you know what time it is?"

"Yes. It's time for you to let me in so I can watch the house while you sleep."

It was then she noticed the overnight bag in his hand and the determined glint in his eyes.

"I thought I made it pretty clear at the restaurant that I don't need you to protect me."

He walked in, placing his overnight bag on the floor before closing the door. His eyes travelled down her body and stopped abruptly at her right hand, which was still holding the gun.

"Oh, hell no. Is that a Glock? A pink Glock? Give it to me." He held out his hand.

She reluctantly handed him the gun. He checked to see if it was loaded, then put it on the table next to the staircase.

"Marion gave it to me."

"Do you even know how to use it? Do you have a license for it?" Michael asked.

"Yes to both questions. Marion taught me how a couple of years ago."

"When did you last fire it?"

"Why do you want to know? I can shoot the damn gun." Anne threw her head back defiantly and placed her hands on her hips.

"When was the last time you shot it?"

"Okay, it's been a while, but one of the deputies offered to take me to the gun range. I think I'll take him up on his offer. I could probably use the practice."

"*I'll* take you to the gun range," he said through gritted teeth. The muscle at the side of his jaw tightened. There was no way he'd let some horny deputy take her to the damn gun range.

She looked down at the overnight bag again. "You're *not* staying."

"Yes, I am."

"I'm not one of those whiny females who's afraid of her own shadow. I don't need you or any other man coming to my rescue. I can take care of myself."

"Where's Hank?"

"He's in Benton County checking out some wind farms."

"Where's Daisy?"

"In Ohio. Her sister broke her arm. Daisy will be there a couple of weeks helping with her sister's kids."

"Where's Harley?"

"Daisy took him with her to entertain the kids."

"It might have been a good idea for Harley to stay here with you. He's a good watch dog with a loud bark." He narrowed his gaze on her face. "So you're the only one here?"

She just shrugged and looked away. "Michael, you are *not* staying. I can protect myself."

"What's wrong with letting someone help you?"

"I don't need help."

"Yes, you do."

"No, I don't, so you can leave." She opened the front door but he didn't budge. "I mean it. I don't need for you to rescue or protect me. I'm a big girl." She picked up his overnight bag, walked out to the porch and placed it on the floor. She stood there glaring at him with her arms crossed over her breasts.

"Have it your way." He joined her on the porch and picked up the bag. "Lock up after I leave."

"No problem." She marched inside, closed the door and twisted the lock.

She sat on the stairs waiting to hear his truck engine roar to life. Instead she heard a scratching then sliding sound at the door lock. She gasped when Michael strode back inside and dropped his overnight bag to the floor.

"How did you…" She jumped to her feet.

"That's how freaking safe your front door is. Anyone with a credit card and half a brain could get in." He scowled at her as he closed the door.

Her eyes darted from him to the door. Fear crept in again, and she blinked watery tears from her eyes. It was back, the same bone-freezing panic she'd had when he left her house the night of the carjacking. Could she really protect herself? It had been years since she'd fired the gun, and she'd only done it once with Marion. She'd had no practice using it, not that she'd share that information with Michael.

"I'll show you the guest room." She looked at him a moment, then picked up her Glock and started up the stairs.

Her blue eyes were so wide and watery it made his chest hurt. Michael wanted to pull her into his arms and hold her. But then he thought of how she'd probably scratch his eyes out if he tried. So he followed her up the stairs instead. She led him down a long hallway, past her bedroom, to a room three doors down. She opened the door and he threw his bag on a small bed.

"The bathroom is down the hall," she offered avoiding his eyes. So she'd let him stay. That didn't mean she had to like it.

"Thanks." He tucked a stray strand of hair behind her ear. "Why don't you try to get some sleep?"

She backed away from his touch then headed toward her bedroom. She closed the door and leaned against it. She imagined how it would feel if his arms were tightly wound around her and pushed the thought out of her head as quickly as it arrived.

Michael removed the quilt from the small bed in the guest room, grabbed the pillow and his bag and went back downstairs to the living room. He created a makeshift bed on the sofa nearest the front door.

He then pulled his 45 caliber out of the bag, slipped it in the back of his jeans and walked through the house, checking each door and window to make sure it was locked.

Sleep was not something she could attain no matter how hard she tried. Once she managed to drift off, the nightmares that came and went were horrible, vivid scenes of how the killer would find her, kill her and leave her body in a cornfield to rot. She'd wake up in a panicky sweat, and then fall back asleep to have the same bad dream again and again.

She went downstairs to the kitchen around three o'clock, made some chamomile tea, and was almost to the stairs when she noticed Michael sleeping on the sofa in the living room. She quietly laid her tea cup on a table and crept into the room. He was sleeping in his clothes with his gun lying close by on a table.

She watched him sleep, his chest moving up and down. She heard his even breathing. She felt a need deep inside and suddenly wanted nothing more than to get him out of his clothes and pull him as close to her as she could. She bit her lip and backed out of the room. She picked up the tea cup and headed back upstairs to her bedroom.

She slipped into a dream where she was lying in bed with Michael. Her arms and legs were wrapped tightly around his body and she felt safer than she'd ever felt. He kissed her until she forgot everything she feared.

Shards of sunlight cut through the shutters. She looked at phone to see it was seven o'clock. She got out of bed.

She washed her face and brushed her teeth in the bathroom. She put on some eye shadow, brushed mascara on her lashes, then smoothed some lip gloss on her mouth. She slipped on a blue T-shirt and a pair of faded jeans. She tied her hair in a ponytail, pulled on her Reeboks, and headed down the stairs.

She saw dark coffee bubbling into the pot when she entered

the kitchen. The bold, rich scent of it drifted in the air. She watched Michael trade the pot with his mug, then back again.

He took a sip and noticed her for the first time. She was leaning against the counter across the room and stared at him until their eyes met. A vaguely sensuous light passed between them. She boldly looked him up and down.

In faded jeans and a tight navy T-shirt, he stood there with his dark looks and rippling muscles looking like a model in a men's cologne ad—radiating sexy masculinity. God, he had an amazing body.

She was an idiot. She'd been burning with lust for him for months, yet pushing him away time and again. What had she been thinking? So what if he'd been Allan's attorney? So what if he had initially believed Allan's lies. She had for years.

She'd never dated, let alone slept with anyone like Michael. The man was sizzling hot. And he hadn't exactly made it a secret that he wanted her.

He watched her carefully across the room. He had never wanted a woman like he wanted her. She had to know that. She had to know what she was doing to him. His need to press that sweet, soft body against his was so strong it was painful. And sleeping in the same house the night before hadn't helped.

She crossed the room until she was standing so close she could feel the heat from his body. She slowly moved her fingers through her hair and removed the elastic band that held her ponytail. She shoved it in her pocket. Her soft hair flowed about her shoulders. She watched a dark gleam come to his eyes. Something heated inside her that made it hard to breathe. Her pulse raced and she wondered if he could hear her heart beat.

He knew that look—that slow burn in her eyes.

"Don't look at me that way," he whispered. "Unless you're going to do something about it."

His pulse spiked as she spread her fingers across his chest and leaned into him until she was pressing her soft breasts against the hardness of his chest. Her eyes, now smoldering, never left his. Then she went on her toes, entangled her fingers in his hair, and pulled him down into a kiss.

Her lips moved gently against his, teasing with her tongue until he felt hot lust shooting through his veins. Her mouth tasted hot and soft. He made a knot in her hair with his hand and parted her lips so he could taste that sweet woman taste he remembered.

He pulled her hard against him and kissed her deeply until she felt the heat of it all the way to her toes. She wrapped her arms around his waist so she could feel the tight muscles in his back that tensed under her touch. She tugged at his shirt and he stopped what he was doing to yank it off. She felt his hot, bare chest against her and tried to pull him closer.

He put his big hands on her bottom and pulled her closer, aligning her body with the hard ridge in his jeans. He pulled her into a deep kiss and glided his hands over her arms, her hips, and she was drowning in dizzying, whirling, heated pleasure. She wished it would never end.

A vibration in his jean pocket jerked them apart. He pulled out his cell phone. His grip tightened around her waist and his expression told her not to move.

"Brandt," he growled. That the interruption angered him was obvious. "Switch the appointment to tomorrow and hold my calls. I'll be in later today. There's something important I need to attend to." He slid the phone across the counter and stared at her. The gleam in his eyes told her what he needed to attend to.

She trailed a finger down the center of his chest, and then moved back slightly to pull on the bottom of her shirt until she lifted it over her head and threw it to the floor. Heat sparked in his eyes. The next thing she knew, his fingers moved over the lavender lace of her bra, cupping her breasts with his big hands as he kissed, licked and teased, building a fire within her that raged at his touch.

Michael lifted her and she wrapped her legs around his waist. He moved through the hallway, then through the door of the formal living room, and set her down on the soft red Oriental rug in front of the fireplace. He locked the door behind them.

He watched as she slowly slid her hands to her back, loosened her bra and sent it to the floor. She then unbuttoned her jeans, slid the zipper down and shimmied out of them until she was wearing only the lavender lace panties.

"I want you." Her voice was low and husky, but she was feeling self-conscious and wished he would hurry before she lost her nerve.

His eyes locked on her as he reached back to pull the gun out of his waistband, and place it on an end table. He threw his wallet on the floor. He pulled his boots off and set them aside one-by-one beside the door. He pulled her into his arms and moved his hands over her waist and hips. He had wanted to touch her for so long, and now he could.

Suddenly he was kissing her thoroughly and she was kissing him back. Her heart felt like it would beat out of her chest with anticipation.

He lowered her to the floor and planted a knee between her knees then leaned over her, bracing his weight on his arms. Ah, she thought, the delicious weight of him. She began to move her hips against him, wanting him, needing him. His mouth moved over hers, this time sending her senses into overload. God, she loved the feel of him, the intensity of his kisses, the way he was touching her. The musky, male scent of him was making her crazy. She tightened her arms around him, pressing against him. She couldn't get enough of him. She wanted him. Now.

His head lifted above hers as he braced himself on his arms. "Are you sure about this, Anne?"

"Yes." She pulled his mouth to hers and kissed him roughly with all of the passion, lust and frustration she'd been holding back for so long.

He leaned on one arm, gazing down at her as he reached for his wallet, removed a foil packet, opened it and covered himself. Please hurry, she thought. She couldn't wait another second. When he shifted over her, she arched her hips up to meet him as he pushed inside her. She gasped at the force of it. He pulled back and did it again, making a low groan in his chest.

She moved her hips against him and he picked up the perfect pace. Their bodies grew slick with sweat. She kissed him, bit at him, clutched his back as he pushed and pushed into her. All she could do was to wrap her legs around him and hold on.

There was nothing but the two of them in this hot, slick dance she wished would never end. He pulled his head back and looked into her eyes. She felt the white-hot heat in her core, and it was building and building until she exploded with pleasure. Moments later, he made a violent thrust and shuddered against her.

He rolled over, taking her with him, holding her in place with her butt in one large hand, and held her head against his chest with the other. She could hear him breathing hard, as if he had just run a couple of miles. Like his, her heart was thundering inside her chest.

What had just happened was something she had never experienced before. She'd been married for years, but making love with Allan was nothing in comparison to this. Michael had set every cell in her body on fire.

His breathing slowed to a normal pace and she rolled to the side and ran her eyes down his naked body. He was perfect—six foot five inches of muscled perfection. She loved everything about his body from the strong arms that held her, to his amazingly gentle, big hands, and all the delicious rest of him. Just looking at him made her hot.

There was just one thing he could improve upon. The post-coital experience could use some work. He was sleeping. Sleeping! So much for pillow talk or cuddling.

Irked, she got up and quietly moved about the room collecting her clothing, then headed for the stairs to get to her bathroom for a shower. She ran the hot water until the room was filled with steam.

She worked shampoo into her hair, and then leaned her head back under the stream of water rinsing the suds away. Without warning, the shower curtain was ripped back and a very naked Michael climbed in.

"Hey!" Her heart leaped and she quickly covered her breasts with her arms.

"Hey, yourself. Move over." He gently pulled her arm down and let his eyes move over her breasts with appreciation. He then kissed her until heat flowed in her veins down to her core. She pushed against his chest then looked up at him.

"I thought you were asleep." She slapped his arm and turned around.

"Yeah, I know you did." He tightened his arms around her shoulders and turned her around so that he was under the water then he whispered in her ear. "Honey, I was taking a short break. We are not even close to being done."

He poured some shower gel into his hand then smoothed it on Anne's arms and breasts, making gentle, sensuous circles until he made a frothy foam coating. A citrusy scent filled the air. He then moved to her back and washed and massaged it as he held her close to his chest. She stretched like a cat and almost purred. He turned her around then knelt to kiss her belly button, then rubbed the sudsy gel onto her long legs, massaging as he went.

His hands were slow and deliberate, igniting a need deep in her that kindled brighter when she met his gaze. She took the shower gel from him and began washing him starting with his back. He reached around grabbing her hips to pull her closer. On her tiptoes, she nibbled on his ear as she massaged his shoulders and arms, receiving a groan from deep in his chest as a reward. She moved around him and gently pushed him under the water, the suds streaming down his body. She then filled her hands with gel and went to work on his chest and pecs. Her hands moved downward to his stomach, massaging with the gel; her fingers making gentle, circular motions. She slid her hand down and smiled at the very male moan he made as she touched him.

He yanked her into his arms, and then using the length of his hard body, pressed her against the cool tile of the shower wall, kissing her with urgency and desperation as if he couldn't get enough of her. She wound her arms around his neck and moved her hips against him, needing him, wanting him again. His hands entangled in her hair, he kissed her again and again, making her crazy with desire.

He turned off the shower, grabbed some towels, scooped her up in his arms and headed for her bed. He laid her down then shifted himself over her, pinning her to the bed with his hips. She sighed and wound her arms around his neck. His kiss tasted all male and Michael. She wanted to drink him in. She arched her hips as he pushed inside her. She moaned and all but screamed his name as he pushed and pushed, her nerves exploding. Each thrust rocked them and brought them closer to the white-hot flame that engulfed them.

They lay together for a while, spent. He propped his weight on his elbows and looked down at her, his eyes dark and serious.

"You know I won't let anything happen to you, don't you?"

Before she could respond, they were both startled by the slamming of a car door in the driveway. Michael moved to the window.

"It's the sheriff." He picked up his jeans and pulled them on then did the same with his boots. She found his shirt on the side of the bed and threw it to him. "I'll make more coffee. Throw some clothes on and come down."

He leaned over to kiss her forehead then raced down the stairs to the front door.

She grabbed some underwear, shirt and jeans from the bureau and moved into the bathroom to dress.

Midway down the stairs, she heard Michael's and Sheriff Miller's voices from the kitchen. She moved to the bottom of the stairs, sat down, and listened.

"My budget was cut this year. I can't spare a deputy to watch her house. I can make sure a deputy looks in while on his regular route, but that's it." Sheriff Miller watched Michael over the edge of his coffee cup.

"Let me see if I can do something out of my budget."

"What's going on between you and her? Are you doing her?"

"That's none of your damn business." Michael's temper flared.

"I get paid for asking questions. Here's another one. How do you know she didn't write that note herself?"

"That's crazy. Why would she do that?"

"Don't know, but you can expect my request for a search warrant. I want her computer, printer, paper and anything else in her office that looks interesting. I also want a handwriting analysis."

"If you had read the note thoroughly, you would have noticed the reference to 'gift'."

"So what?"

"You and I are the only two people who heard what Doc Meade said about how the ribbon tied around the body could represent a gift. Hell, maybe *you* wrote the note. I know I didn't."

"You might think twice about getting cozy with a suspect. Ethics and all."

At first, Anne hugged her knees to her chest and thought she might get sick. Then anger flickered within her like a fire. Not only was she not going to get protection from a killer, she was considered a suspect. It made no sense.

Michael had defended her to the sheriff. Not only had he defended her, he was putting his job at risk for her, and she'd had no clue. No one had done anything like that for her before. Ever.

She couldn't let him put his job or his career in jeopardy for her. She wouldn't. She didn't even know if she was in love with him. Yes, she loved how he made her feel, but that didn't necessarily mean she was *in* love with him. One thing was for sure, she could never live with herself if it were her fault he lost his job.

She heard the sound of chairs scraping across the floor, then footsteps. She met the sheriff's glare head-on as he passed the stairway. He slammed the front door and she headed back up the stairs.

Ten minutes later in the kitchen, she watched Michael staring out the kitchen window, his hands balled into fists at his hips, and his body rigid with anger.

"How about some breakfast?" She opened the refrigerator and took out eggs, butter, bacon, and bread for toast. He turned around and watched her as she placed several strips of bacon in the skillet and turned up the heat.

"You cook?"

"Sometimes. And don't act so surprised." She cracked an egg, and then put two slices of bread in the toaster.

He opened cabinet doors until he found two plates, then looked in drawers until he found silverware, which he put on the table. He pulled a coffee mug down, filled it and handed it to Anne. He stood behind her, wrapped his arms around her shoulders and kissed her hair and neck.

She smiled, leaned back against him and flipped an egg. This felt so good being with him doing ordinary things. Her throat went dry as she thought of the difficult talk she would have with him soon. Making love with him had made that talk one of the hardest she'd ever have to do. He'd probably hate her and never touch her again.

She filled their plates, took them to the table then swung back to the refrigerator for butter and jam for the toast.

She spread butter on her toast and watched Michael dig in. She waited until he'd finished his eggs and was on his third cup of coffee before she spoke.

"What did the sheriff have to say?"

"Nothing much. There's still no suspect in the Rachel Mitchell case."

So that was the laundered version. Obviously, he didn't want her to know everything the sheriff had to say—like the part about their relationship and ethics.

She took their plates to the sink.

"Are you still going to your office?"

"Yes, for a couple of hours."

"Okay, I'll walk you to the door."

Chapter 7

She knew the exact second Michael noticed his packed duffle bag by the front door. His expression registered surprise, then a spark of anger lit his eyes, and his jaw tensed.

"What's going on?" Hands on his hips, he looked down at her with one of his more intimidating glares.

"I agreed to your staying over for *one* night. I can take care of myself from this point on." The words came out sounding calm, but her nerves were raw. If her heart pounded any harder, it would jump right out of her chest.

"Yeah, you did a bang-up job of taking care of yourself that night you got carjacked." His words stung, and he didn't seem to care.

"You can't stay here, Michael."

"Why not?"

"It's just not a good idea."

"Why isn't it?" He scanned her face as if he was trying to read her mind, and she sincerely hoped he couldn't. Her words were stumbling and she didn't know what to say next.

"Because the sheriff will make sure I'm protected." She knew this was a lie, but threw it out there anyway.

"Yeah, sure he will. There's no money in his budget, Anne. No witness protection. Not in the cards. So you've got me. *I'm* your protection."

"No. I'm not ready for you to stay here." It was another lie, but she was running out of phony excuses for him to stay away.

"Why not?"

"I'm not ready to get involved." Damn. Why did she say that?

"Oh, really, you seemed more than ready to get involved in the living room a couple of hours ago." He was livid. He stepped toward her and she stepped back.

"Well, that was..." God, she was tripping over her thoughts again.

"Oh, and don't forget the shower, then your bed. Yeah, I'd say you were ready to get involved those times too."

"Michael, please just leave. We can't see each other for a while."

"How long is 'a while'?"

"Listen. You're a prosecutor. I know there are probably rules about you seeing someone who plays a role in an active investigation. So I don't think we should see each other until after Rachel's killer is caught and you've prosecuted him."

"Seriously? Do you know how long that could take?" He was incredulous. It sometimes took years to apprehend, let alone prosecute a killer.

"I want you to send him away, Michael, so he can't hurt anyone else. You *can't* let him get off on some technicality. That just can't happen. I need you to do this for me." Anne knew she was right. She heard he was a pit bull in court. The killer would be put away for a long, long time if Michael had anything to do with it. She also knew if the killer got away on a technicality because of something he did, it might destroy him.

A lone tear streamed down her cheek and she quickly wiped it away.

"What if I can't?"

"Can't what?"

"Stay away." He opened the front door, grabbed his duffel bag and left.

She gulped hard, hot tears flowing down her face. She could never, never let him know she was doing this to protect his career. She knew he wouldn't stand for it. She could not let his need to protect her put everything he'd worked so hard for at risk. No matter how much it hurt.

She wrapped her arms around herself and wondered if she would ever see him again.

She pulled her cell phone out of her pocket and called Hank. Within minutes, they sat together at the dining room table.

"As it turns out, the body that was dumped in our field, Rachel Mitchell was not there by accident," said Anne.

"What?"

"Someone left it there and sent me a note that leads me to believe I'm his next target. The sheriff doesn't have money in the budget for protection, so we need to do something ourselves."

"Holy shit. Are you sure?"

"Unfortunately, yes."

"Okay. Here's something I can do right away. I'll meet with the farmhands; they need to know about this. They can help by making sure their hunting guns are registered and on the gun racks in their trucks. There's no reason they can't be armed when they come to work."

"Okay. There's another thing. I want you to work with Rick Davies, who will be here to do a security assessment on the farm, house and barn. Just give him a tour of the property and brief me on what security should be added, and we'll go from there."

"I'll watch for him. In the meantime, I'm going to the barn to talk to the farmhands."

Anne joined Hank and Rick Davies in the kitchen where Rick had brochures and papers spread across the round oak table. She glanced at Hank. She might be imagining it, but Hank seemed to sit a little taller since morning. She wondered if his new confidence had to do with her asking him to help with security.

"I've listened to Rick's security recommendations and think we should start by securing the driveway with a gate equipped with a key pad and phone." Hank slid the assessment over to Anne.

Rick glanced at Hank, and then turned his attention to Anne. "We can install the key pad so that it is reachable from a truck or car window. Let's put the phone in for people who don't have a code, but may have business at the farm." He watched Anne as she glanced over the assessment and hoped she would sign off on it. Thanks to his brother's proclivity for breaking the law, he owed

Michael Brandt more than a couple of favors. He'd shaved off around 40% of what he regularly charged customers.

Hank added, "We can limit access to staff, family and friends. I also like Rick's idea to install a web-based surveillance system so that you and I can monitor the property remotely on our computers. Images of anyone entering or leaving the property will be saved and we can play them back."

Rick added, "I suggest you install weatherproof security cameras at the gate, four corners of the house and barn."

"Along with the cameras, I'll install motion detector flood light," said Rick.

Anne nodded and gazed at her farm manager. "Hank, what do you think?"

"The cost is fair, Anne. We need the security."

"To think I believed I would be safer by moving here, away from the city." She sighed and looked at both men, who waited for her decision. "Make it happen."

"We can make it happen, but it will be at least a month, maybe more," said Rick. "Just want you to know that before we get started."

The Chambers Restaurant was a popular watering hole across from the courthouse, and had the best ribs in town. It was close to one o'clock and as usual, it was packed with the lunch crowd of attorneys, courthouse employees and cops.

Michael watched as the tall blonde woman entered the bar. She spotted him and sashayed up to the bar. She was wearing a red wrap dress that highlighted her curves, which were not unnoticed by a table of men sitting near the door.

When she reached Michael, he stood to shake her hand, which meant this meeting was business and he had an assignment for her.

"So you need my services again?" She sat on the bar stool and crossed her legs.

"Yes, Douglas Investigations is on the top of my list for private investigation. How are you, Frankie? Still like apple martinis?"

"Ah, you remembered."

While he looked for the bartender, she checked him out, noting how good the man looked in jeans. Usually, they met in his office and he wore a suit. He looked good in a suit. But looking at him in these body-hugging jeans, her heartbeat kicked up a notch. He was smokin' hot.

He gazed at her for a moment. "This job is a little different from your assignments in the past."

"How different?"

"I have a witness I want you to keep an eye on."

He waved the bartender over and ordered an apple martini for her and another Coors for himself. She watched him, wondering who the witness was who had him drinking his lunch.

"Homicide case?"

"Yes. I have reason to believe the killer is targeting her."

"Who's after her? Who's your suspect?"

"Don't have one," said Michael.

"Can't you put her in protective custody?"

"No, there's no money in the budget to do that."

This meant he was covering her expenses on this assignment himself. Again, she wondered who the witness was. "Understood. What do you want me to do?"

"Tail her and cover her at her house. I don't want her out of your sight. But I don't want her to know you're watching her. Do you understand?"

"Yeah, I get it. What's her name?"

"Anne Mason. She owns Golden Acres Farm."

"Isn't that the woman who found Rachel Mitchell's body in her cornfield? I read the story in the paper."

"That's her."

"Are you telling me that Rachel's killer is now after Anne Mason?"

"Yes."

"When do you want me to start?" Frankie couldn't read his expression. She couldn't tell if he was pissed, or just really worried about this woman. She also wondered exactly what his relationship was with Anne Mason.

"Now." He chugged the rest of his beer and set the bottle on the bar. "Right freaking now. And keep me updated." He slapped a twenty-dollar bill on the bar. She watched him leave, then pulled her cell phone out of her purse and Googled Anne Mason.

Michael stared blankly out his office window. He felt like his brain was scrambled and he was having trouble making sense of things. How could his day have gone from the best he'd ever had, to the worst, in only a matter of hours? He kept reliving making love to Anne and how she'd responded. She practically burst into flames from the first moment he touched her this morning. Then his mind went to the front door, seeing his packed bag and recalling the conversation that had ended with "we can't see each other." How had things gotten so screwed up?

His secretary knocked on his door then popped her head in. "I know you told me you didn't want to be disturbed, but you've got a call from Helen Anderson. Do you want to take it?"

"Put it through."

"Hi, Helen. How is our new State Attorney?" He'd known Helen for a decade. It was Helen who had urged him when he was a cop to go to law school. It was Helen who was his mentor.

"I'm hearing rumors, Michael."

"What kind of rumors?"

"I'm hearing you are in a personal relationship with a witness in an active investigation."

"I'm guessing Sheriff Miller told you that." The trouble-making bastard moved fast.

"It doesn't matter who told me. Is it true?" Her tone kicked up a notch. She sounded annoyed.

"It was until she kicked me out this morning. Doesn't want to see me until after the killer is caught and the trial is over." He'd always been nothing but honest with Helen. He wasn't going to start lying now. Although a part of him wanted to.

"Smart girl."

"A trial could be years away. I don't know if I can stay away from her."

"Is it that serious?"

"For me, it is."

"Damn it. Don't do something you'll regret. You've worked so hard to get where you are, Michael. Don't screw it up."

"Thanks for the advice. Is that all?"

He slammed the receiver down and scrubbed his hands across his face. In his career, he'd kept his professional behavior clean as a whistle. No complications. Now he found himself knee-deep in something that was beyond complicated.

He had this overwhelming need to protect a woman who didn't want protecting. Okay, it was more than that. There was a good chance he was more than half-way in love with the most stubborn, distrusting, intelligent and sexiest woman he'd ever met. And if he did what she asked, there was a good chance he'd lose her. But if he did what he wanted to do, what he needed to do, he could very well lose his career.

He pulled out his keys and locked the desk. He had to get out of there before he started breaking things. He headed to the gym where he lifted weights for an hour. After a hot shower, he got in his truck for the drive home. He hadn't gone far, before he realized he hadn't heard from his private investigator.

"Frankie, what's going on?"

"Plenty. Which part do you want to hear about, the field mouse that tried to crawl up my pants or what your witness is up to?"

"Is she okay?"

"Yeah. I'm at her farm in the cornfield. I can see her right now through binoculars. And if I see another field mouse, I'm going to shoot its head off."

"Why are you in the field?"

"Had to hide my car and this was the closest I could get to the house." She paused as she adjusted her position. "She's got a visitor. Arrived about an hour ago."

"Who is it?"

"It's Lane Hansen. Just ran his plates. If you want a description, he looks like he could play quarter-back for the Indianapolis Colts."

"Name sounds familiar."

"It should. He's a deputy. Works for Sheriff David E. Miller."

When she heard no response, she looked at her phone. He had disconnected the call. Nice mood he was in today. She picked up the binoculars and peered through them.

Michael gritted his teeth. Just when he thought this crap day couldn't get worse. Lane Hansen? Yeah, his name was familiar all right. He was one of the deputies eyeing Anne the day she found the body. Shit.

The next thing Frankie saw from her binoculars was Michael's silver Escalade EXT racing down the lane toward the house. What the hell was going on?

He parked behind the blue Dodge Ram he assumed belonged to Hansen. He leapt from his truck and was about to slam the door when he heard gunshots coming from the back of the house. He dove into the front seat and grabbed his revolver from the glove box.

When he reached the back yard, he saw Anne pointing her pink Glock at a round, black and white paper target mounted on a fence. Her arms were extended, feet spread, hands aiming the gun at the target. He watched as Hansen moved behind her, smoothing his hands down her arms to adjust her aim. His jaw clenched. The sight of Hansen touching her made him want to rip his head off.

Anne shot at the target nearly hitting the bull's eye.

"Hey, not bad, Anne!"

She turned to say something to Hansen when she noticed Michael leaning against the side of the house. Even from the distance, she could see his expression was a perfect storm of jealousy, anger and testosterone. He beamed a take-no-prisoners glare at the deputy's back.

"Hi, Michael. Did you bring the legal papers with you?" That was the only excuse she could invent for him being there. Damn it. He was supposed to stay away. The last thing they needed was to be the focus of deputy gossip.

Hansen turned around and waved. He watched Michael as he headed toward them.

"I took Lane up on his offer to teach me to shoot." Anne explained, keeping her tone friendly.

"I can see that." He accepted Hansen's offer to shake hands.

Then he gritted his teeth and put his hands on his hips.

"How are you doing?" He scowled down at Anne, looking very pissed. The way his eyes moved down her body told her, he wasn't just talking about her aim.

"Okay. No bull's eyes yet, but some close hits."

"Let's see you try it again." He watched as she faced the target with a wide stance, two-handed grip and steady aim. He moved in back of her as Hansen had done, but when he touched her, his hands possessively gripped her waist.

"Take a deep breath and fill your lungs with air. Hold it. Then shoot." He ran his hands down her hips. Something very warm was shooting through her system. She nearly gasped when he tugged her against his hard body. "Are you ready?"

"What?" The heat of his body made it hard to focus. She tried to wiggle out of his grip without calling attention to it. No luck.

"When you're ready to shoot, do it."

She shot and the target flipped wildly. Hansen ran to the fence to get it. He held it up and called, "bull's eye!"

Changing the subject and activity seemed like a good idea, so she told Michael about Rick Davies' security assessment.

"Glad you're going with his recommendations. When did he say he can get it installed?"

"It may take a month or more. In fact, that was one of the things Lane and I were just talking about."

"Is that so?" So it was Lane, now. What happened to "Deputy" Hansen? Since when were they on a first name basis?

"Lane agreed to do surveillance at the house at night until the security system gets installed."

"Really?" He turned to the deputy. "When I talked to your boss, he said there was no money in the budget for surveillance." His eyes narrowed as he watched Hansen.

"Doing it when I'm off duty." He met Michael's glare head on.

"Lane said he could keep a close watch from his truck all night. He'll leave when the farmhands start arriving at dawn."

"No shit. Very kind of you, Lane." Just fucking great. She wouldn't let him stay with her to protect her, but good old Lane gets to stay all night at her place in the truck. The jerk was probably plotting right now how to move surveillance to her bedroom. He knew *he* would be.

"It's just until the security is installed." She noticed that Michael seemed to be getting angrier, if that was possible. It was a good time for him to leave before he did something they'd both regret. "Michael, why don't I walk you to your car so we can get those legal papers?"

After a couple of steps, she felt his big hand pressed against her back. She moved aside and looked back at Hansen who was cleaning her gun.

"Please don't touch me and give the impression we've got something going. You shouldn't be here. We talked about it this morning."

"*You* talked about it. And *we* certainly didn't discuss this. I sure in-the-hell wouldn't have bought into this little arrangement you've got going with Hansen." His glare intensified, so she looked away.

"It's only for a month or so." How in the world were they going to make it through the long haul when they were struggling to make it through the first day?

"Well, don't trust him. And don't let him in the house. He'll make a beeline for your bedroom."

"Oh, really?" She wrapped her arms around herself and wondered if he really thought it would be that easy for Lane Hansen to get into her bed.

"Yes, really." He leaned against his truck watching her closely. The image of Hansen running his hands over her body made him a little sick and a lot pissed.

"You mean like *you* did." She glared at him and scanned his face for his reaction.

"If you think what we have is anything close to what that guy has in mind…" He glared down at her and fought the urge to throw her over his shoulder and take her up to her bedroom and kiss her senseless.

"Forget it. Do you have a paper in your truck you can hand me? Lane is watching us."

In the cornfield, darkness moved in and Frankie pulled the hood of her sweatshirt up as a chilly burst of wind sent a chill through her body. She wore a camouflage jumpsuit with a brown hoodie. Tomorrow night's weather was predicted to be colder so she'd add insulated underwear for more warmth. She pulled out her thermos and sipped the now lukewarm espresso, hoping the caffeine would kick her energy up a level.

Thank goodness for Uncle Sam, she thought. Four years in the Army had toughened her up and taught her the kind of skills that came in handy with watching and chasing bad guys. Marksmanship was her specialty, and she'd earned several awards for her efforts, including sharpshooter medals that were now framed and on her office wall to impress prospective customers.

She had a reputation of handling herself with the toughest, which made growing her private investigative business easier than she thought it would be.

She looked at her sports watch. It was eleven o'clock; she had just sixty minutes left until her partner, Ted, relieved her at midnight. She lucked out with the weather as the sky was clear with a million glittery stars. Visibility was perfect. A city girl, she'd forgotten how peaceful nights could be in the country. Except for the occasional moo of a cow in a nearby field or the breeze that rustled the corn plants, it was quiet.

She focused the binoculars on the window that Michael said was Anne's bedroom. The light was still on.

Anne carried fresh sheets from the linen closet. One look at her disheveled bed had her pulse racing. Sex with Michael had been an athletic event.

She cursed her current circumstances and began stripping her bed, starting with the top sheet. She jerked the pillow case from her pillow and tossed it on the floor with the rest of the bed linen. She reached for the other pillow, then stopped in her tracks. She held the pillow close to her chest and inhaled. It was Michael's scent—citrusy from the shower, all male and all Michael. She buried her face in it for a moment, and then tossed it onto the loveseat. God, she was pathetic. Was she honestly not going to change the pillowcase because it had his scent on it?

With a quick shake of the comforter, she finished making her bed. She washed up in the bathroom, slipped on a blue satin nightshirt then peered out the window to see if Lane Hansen's truck was still parked in the yard.

She assured herself that Lane was there, then crawled into bed, and curled into a fetal position around Michael's pillow.

Frankie watched the light in Anne's upstairs bedroom window go out. She repositioned the binoculars and could see Lane Hansen's truck behind some bushes near the garage. Her back muscles cramped from lying on her stomach too long and she envied Hansen his comfy seat in his truck. She pulled herself up in a yoga position and stretched.

She thought about Michael Brandt and what she'd seen earlier. What she assumed was a simple job of witness surveillance and protection was starting to look a lot more like a personal thing for her boss. Even from a distance through binoculars, she could see how pissed he was with Lane Hansen. One thing was clear, he didn't want Hansen there. This was a little confusing since he'd hired her to do the same thing Hansen was doing. Why wasn't he glad to have another professional watching over his witness?

The more she thought about it, the more she was sure protection for this particular witness was personal for Michael.

From what she'd heard about him, Michael Brandt didn't linger long with one woman, and there had been many. Women threw themselves at him, always had. Hell, she'd done it herself and was more than disappointed there had been no interest on his part. She didn't know if he had something going with this woman, but she was sure Anne Mason was more than a witness to him. She didn't plan to ask him about it though, because she knew she'd get one of his none-of-your-freaking-business glares. No thank you very much.

A crunching sound from the right jerked her back to reality. Something a lot heavier than field mouse made that noise. She slowly stretched out on her stomach, pushed the binoculars to her eyes, aiming them toward the sound. She could make out a man in a crouching position. He was wearing a light gray hoodie and was holding binoculars that were aimed toward the house. She estimated he was about fifteen or so rows away. Shit. Was he the killer? Suddenly she realized if she could see him, he could see her if he turned his attention her way.

She quietly moved her right hand down to the holster at her waist and pulled out her revolver. She slowly and soundlessly turned around, and then did an army crawl twenty feet or so. She bent down, found his image in her binoculars in the same position. Crouching, she moved back a few more feet then started crossing the field toward what she guessed was his row counting as she went. She reached the fifteenth row of corn, turned and moved. She said a silent prayer that she got the drop on him, before he even realized he was not alone in the field.

As she drew closer, she realized he was about five rows over from her initial guesstimate. He was still in a crouching position, holding the binoculars close to his eyes as he watched the house.

She did some slow sidesteps, choosing wider spaces between corn plants until she was standing in his row. Without a sound, she crept up behind him, stopping when she was within two feet of him. She raised her revolver to assume a firing position,

"Make one move and I'll shoot your freaking head off."

He jerked, dropped the binoculars then spun around and slammed into her. Her gun exploded before sailing into the night as she fell with him on top of her. His fist slammed into her face, but not before she could get in a knee to his groin. She knew her knee had made contact when he bent over and started howling. Her face was on fire with pain and blood sprayed from her mouth and nose. She jumped to her feet and kicked him hard in the stomach and heard him grunt and gasp for air. She bent to the ground, her hands searching the earth frantically for her gun. He recovered, grabbed her by the hair, and threw her to the ground where she hit her head hard. She saw him grab the binoculars and heard his feet hitting the ground as he ran away. She struggled to get to her feet to give chase, but something wet was in her eyes and she couldn't see. She sank to the ground, holding her throbbing head in her hands and wiping at her eyes.

She heard someone running toward her from a different direction and she prayed it was her partner, Ted. She could see a wide strip of light from a flashlight wave back and forth until it reached her. She blinked until she realized she was looking into the barrel of a revolver.

"You move. You're dead." His voice was a low growl and was definitely not Ted's. Deputy Lane Hansen stood over her. Holy shit.

"Don't shoot," she got out. "Let me get in my pocket so I can show you my I.D." God, it hurt to move.

"I heard a gunshot. Where's the gun?"

"He knocked it out of my hand. I can't find it. Please, let me get my ID."

"Do it. Any funny stuff, buddy, and you'll regret it. I guarantee it."

She looked up at the gun then him and pulled out her identification and handed it to him. Deputy Hansen focused his flashlight on it and read.

"Frankie Douglas. You're a P.I.? What the hell are you doing out here?" He shoved his gun back in the holster and yanked her up by the back of her sweatshirt. Her long blonde hair tumbled to her shoulders when she reached her feet.

"Christ, you're a woman?"

"Very perceptive of you to notice." Damn. How more embarrassing was this going to get? First, her mark gets the drop on her and beats the living crap out her. Now, Deputy Lane Hansen was sure to grill her about what was going on, and would totally blow her cover. Nice night's work.

He pulled her toward him by the front of her sweatshirt to get a better look, focusing his flashlight on her face. "You're bleeding."

"No kidding. Good detective work." She used the arm of her sweatshirt to wipe at her cheek.

"Come on, wiseass. You're coming to my truck to get your face taken care of and then you're going to tell me what the hell just happened out here." He grabbed her by the arm and half drug her to his truck, ignoring her curses and demands to walk on her own.

When they got to his truck, he opened the passenger side and held the door as she got in. He stood there for a moment glaring at her, then slammed the door and walked around the truck to get in the driver's side.

He reached across her and she stiffened, pressing her back against the seat. "I'm just getting into the glove box for the first aid kit. Relax. Haven't decided if I'm going to arrest you yet."

"What? You've got to be kidding." The situation was getting worse and worse. She could hear the gossip now. And there was nothing worse than the cop grapevine. Her reputation was going to be toast.

He turned on the interior light, opened the first aid kit and started pulling out gauze, alcohol pads, Band-Aids, and some ointment. It gave her a chance to really look at him. The man was huge without a fat cell in his body. She hadn't been exaggerating before when she told Michael he could have played for the Colts.

"Take off your sweatshirt."

"Excuse me?" She didn't care how big he was, she was *not* going to start taking off her clothes.

"Take it off or I will. I need to see your injuries."

His hard, determined expression told her he would not hesitate to rip the sweatshirt off her body. She slowly unzipped it and pulled her arms through the sleeves revealing the brown camisole underneath. When she set the sweatshirt in her lap, she noticed it was wet with blood that spattered the front. Her blood. She looked at Hansen who was doing a good job of checking out her breasts.

He turned her around and leaned in to study her face. "Bet it was quite a fight. Who won?"

She gave him her most hateful scowl, which he ignored as he held her chin. He wiped at the blood with some gauze, and then peeled back the foil on an alcohol pad.

"Damn it. Do you have to use that? It's going to hurt like hell."

"Yes, I have to use it. It will hurt more if those cuts get infected. Hold still and quit acting like a baby."

Sadist. He was probably enjoying this. And, she did *not* act like a baby. She was right about the pain. It took all the self-control she had not to shriek each time he dabbed a cut with the pad. He followed with some ointment, then leaned back to look at her again.

"You're going to have a shiner."

"Great. I've got a new dress that will match it."

"That will do it for your face. What about your other injuries? Maybe you better take off your shirt and pants."

"Oh, hell no. We're through playing doctor, Deputy Hansen."

"You know my name?"

"Lucky guess."

"No, it's not. How do you know my name? Have we met?" Even though he asked the last question, there was no way they'd met. He would have remembered those whiskey-brown eyes, blonde hair, full breasts, and tight body.

Something vibrated against her hip and she pulled her cell phone out of her hip pocket. It was Ted. "I need to get this." He nodded and she slid out of the passenger seat, closed the door and leaned against the truck feeling Hansen's glare on her back.

"Hey, where are you?"

"I ran into a situation. I'm dealing with it now."

"What kind of situation?"

"Can't talk now. I'll call you later."

She got back into the truck and glanced at Hansen who was drumming his fingers impatiently on the steering wheel.

"Let's start by talking about what you were doing in the field."

"I recently took up astronomy. Did you notice how bright the Little Dipper is tonight?"

"You're a real comedian, aren't you? Since you're a P.I., my guess is someone hired you to keep an eye on Anne Mason. You need to tell me who."

"I'm sorry, but that's confidential information."

"Who hired you?" He used his best don't-fuck-with-me glare that usually brought suspects to their knees. It had no effect on her.

"Confidential."

His eyes scanned over her face, noting the squint of her eyes and the set of her jaw. This woman had no fear and the chances he'd get any information out of her was pretty slim. But that didn't mean he wasn't going to try.

"Who'd you shoot at?"

"Don't know. Could have been a corn poacher." She looked at him using her most wide-eyed, innocent look as she shrugged her shoulders.

"Bullshit. And I might add you're getting on my last nerve." He was getting pissed and would have had her flattened on the ground if she'd been a man.

"Sorry about that, deputy," said Frankie, using a sarcastic tone.

That was the last straw. He jerked his seat back and hauled her over the console so she landed on his lap with a gasp. She pushed against his chest to make some space between them. A current of lust shot through him and he pulled her into a kiss.

It was supposed to be a punishing kiss but once he tasted the blood from the cuts on her lips, he probed her mouth gently. Her mouth felt hot, soft and very female. He wrapped his heavy arms around her to pull her closer.

Warmth flowed through her blood and Frankie leaned into the kiss, winding her arms around his neck. She couldn't remember the last time a kiss felt this good. She let her tongue flicker inside his mouth. He moaned and pulled at her leg so that she sat straddling him. Crap. What was she doing? What was she thinking? She pulled her head back. Their gazes locked and a spark of heat flashed between them.

"I think we should stop now, don't you officer?"

"Nope, and I'm off-duty."

She pushed herself back to the passenger seat. "Oh, really? So that threat earlier about arresting me was pretty much bullshit, right?"

"No more bullshit than the weak stories you've been giving me."

She yanked open the truck door and slammed it soundly. Asshole. He was a good example of why she didn't date cops. Bullshitting and downright lying came too damn easy for them. Damn Lane Hansen anyway. And he better not tell his cop pals how someone got the drop on her in the field. Damn him. And where did he learn to kiss like that anyway?

He watched her walk away, while pushing a couple of buttons on his cell phone. "Hey, Sally, I heard you were working nights now. Honey, I need a little favor. Would you please get me all you can find on a P.I. named Frankie Douglas?"

She thought she would never find her car. By the time she got to it, she was exhausted and cursed herself for parking it so far away. What a crappy night and now she had to tell her boss just how badly she screwed up. When he found out she'd let his suspect get away, he'd fire her, or worse.

Chapter 8

Frankie sat in Mom's Diner, staring at a breakfast menu, and wondering why the service was so slow this morning. She noticed a round table of five cops who were hooting and hollering about some joke one of them told. At least, she hoped it was a joke and not a re-enactment of what happened to her last night. What she wouldn't do for a cup of hot coffee. Where was a damn waitress anyway?

She pulled a compact from her purse and peered at herself in the small round mirror. Thanks to four hours of sleep, there were dark smudges under her eyes. She reached in her purse for a tube and smoothed cover-up cream on the dark areas. Bless the lord for cover-up cream and matte makeup. No one would even notice she'd gotten the crap beaten out of her the night before. She'd loaded up on eye shadow, too, in purple like the shade the skin above her eye was turning. Some cherry-red lip gloss and a couple layers of black mascara, and she was good to go.

She checked her clothes, a black pant suit with a sexy ivory lace camisole. Leopard patterned pumps with four inch heels completed her look. It was her good luck outfit. Every time she wore it, good things happened. She was going to need all the luck she could get when she met with Michael Brandt this morning. How was she going to spin what happened last night? How was she going to tell him the perp got away?

Finally, a waitress carrying a full pot of hot coffee headed her way and Frankie turned her coffee mug over to be filled.

"Mornin', darlin'. Looks like you could use a little of this." She filled Frankie's mug, grabbed a handful of creamer containers out of her pocket, tossed them on the table and headed back toward the kitchen.

"Hey, I know what I want to order," called Frankie after her. There was no way this waitress was going to get out of her sight.

"Okay, I'm ready if you are. We're getting quite a crowd this morning." She set the coffee pot on the table and pulled out a small pad from her uniform.

"I'll have scrambled eggs, bacon, and blueberry pancakes with a glass of chocolate milk. And, please keep the coffee coming."

"Got it. Honey, do you want to add a bag of ice for that eye?" She peered down at Frankie with wide eyes filled with sympathy. "No need to be embarrassed. It wasn't that long ago, my prick ex-husband gave me a shiner just like that one."

"No thanks. Just the food and coffee." Well, so much for people not noticing. She shook her head, then poured three containers of cream in her mug and stirred the dark liquid with a spoon. She inhaled a calming breath, exhaled and took her first sip, glancing around the room over the edge of the mug.

She took another sip and noticed a huge man wearing a deputy uniform walk in from the outside. He talked a moment at the cop table, and then scanned the room as if looking for someone. He appeared to target her or maybe someone at a table behind her and moved forward. She grabbed a dessert menu and placed it over her face pretending to study it.

"Imagine meeting you here, Frankie." Lane Hansen pulled the menu out of her hands and tossed it on the table. He dragged out the chair across from her and made himself comfortable.

"Why do I doubt this meeting is accidental?" Damn, he was a giant. He looked much bigger and scarier in the light of day. He was a lot better-looking, too, with blue-gray eyes, lips firm and sensual. His massive shoulders stretched the uniform shirt he wore. Shit. She certainly didn't want to do the interrogation dance with him this early. Especially when she had a meeting with Michael Brandt in an hour that she needed to mentally prepare for.

Two lithe, young waitresses popped out of the kitchen armed with coffee pots. They appeared to be in the Olympics 800 meter sprint to see who could reach Lane Hansen's table first. The dark-haired waitress slid on the hardwood floor then skidded to a stop by Hansen first. She gave the other waitress a victorious smile then filled Hansen's cup. Frankie's eyes squinted with irritation. She'd waited ten minutes to even be noticed.

"Morning, Helen. I'll have my usual. Also, would you do me a favor and bring me a plastic bag filled with ice for my friend here." Frankie glared at him as the waitress scurried back with his order.

"I don't need ice *and* you are *not* my friend."

He just stared at her, letting his eyes study her face then wander over the rest of her. "You're looking hot in that suit, Frankie. I especially like those leopard shoes. But your eye looks nasty."

"Thanks for sharing." She said it in her most sarcastic tone, but it seemed to have been lost on him. He was on a mission. She could see it in his eyes. Or maybe he wasn't—because right now his eyes were roaming over her in a way that was quite un-deputy like.

"I've got something for you." He reached into his pocket, and then slid her revolver across the table. She grabbed it and slipped it in her black leather purse. In a grating falsetto, he mimicked, "Thank you for finding it, Lane. Oh, I noticed you cleaned it for me. Thank you so much."

"Thanks." God, he was annoying. And it wasn't just because it was so early and she was on her first cup of coffee.

"I've got some questions for you." He gave her his scariest look, but she just sat there glaring back at him, so he shot her a threat. "And if I don't get some answers, I have no problem cuffing you and hauling your pretty little ass to the station to answer them."

"I thought we finished this little talk last night." She shot one of her more dazzling smiles at him to distract him and seductively ran her finger across the lace of her camisole revealing the swell of her breasts. It was worth a shot. When he just scowled, she shifted uncomfortably in her chair.

The dark-haired waitress returned with two platters of food and set them in front of the deputy. She dropped a plastic bag filled with ice in front of Frankie.

"Lane, just let me know if you need anything else." She flashed Lane a wide smile and tapped on his napkin with her fingernail.

"Thanks, Helen." He pulled the paper napkin out from under the utensils, fanned it then put it across his lap failing to see the phone number printed in pencil. Frankie rolled her eyes.

"Hungry?" She jabbed at him. Who eats that much food? Frankie gritted her teeth as her stomach growled. Where was *her* food?

"Just worked out. I'm starving." He dug in, scooping eggs and hash browns in his mouth before dipping his toast in the yolk. He picked up a juicy piece of bacon and held it out to her.

She grabbed it, ripped off a piece and shoved in her mouth. She leaned to look around him to see her waitress heading toward her. Finally.

"Here, honey. Sorry it took so long. Oh, I see you got some ice for your eye. You know you might want to lose some weight like I did."

"What?" Frankie looked down, scanning her body and certainly was not seeing any extra flab.

"Yeah, I lost about 200 pounds when I kicked out my ex. No more black eyes for me. You should do the same." She gave Frankie's shoulder a little squeeze then headed for the kitchen. Hansen laughed. She glared.

"Frankie rubbed her temples with the tips of her fingers. Her eye was starting to throb. She rummaged in her purse until she found an Advil in her makeup bag.

"You owe me a piece of bacon." His eyes glittered with amusement.

Could he be any more annoying? Frankie popped the Advil in her mouth and washed it down with chocolate milk. She placed a piece of bacon on his plate then focused on her food. She hadn't eaten since yesterday afternoon. She poured syrup on the pancakes, and then absently licked her sticky fingers. She noted his eyes widen. She'd seen that look before and knew exactly what it was and how it might work to her advantage in the little interrogation she was sure he planned.

Famished, she shoveled in her food. When she finished, she sighed, and leaned back against the seat and stared at Lane Hansen who was staring back at her.

He reached in his back pocket and pulled out a small plastic bag and slid it across the table. Inside were several cigarette butts.

"Where did you get those?"

"I waited until it was light then I searched the field where I found you."

"Is collecting litter in your job description? That's very Boy Scout of you." Panic filled her with tiny pin pricks of fear. Crap. Michael Brandt was going to kill her. Those cigarettes were probably smoked by the bastard watching Anne Mason's house, who was probably the perp who killed the Mitchell girl and wanted to do the same to Anne. Her pulse leapt. She couldn't interfere with an active investigation. She knew that much. She also couldn't reveal that Michael hired her.

"You can save the smartass remarks. Who'd you fight with in the field last night?"

"He didn't introduce himself." She avoided his fierce glare by looking at what was left of her food. She pushed her plate away. She'd lost her appetite.

"How about we make a little trade?"

"What kind of trade?" Her eyes narrowed with distrust. She hadn't forgotten that kiss in his truck. She'd kissed him back, which was a colossal mistake that was not to be repeated. So if he was suggesting some kind of sexual trade, he was going to be disappointed.

"See that table up front filled with cops? They're buddies of mine. I bet they'd enjoy a good story about a certain female P.I., with Army Sharpshooter badges no less, who not only lost her gun but got her ass kicked last night. You know, the upside to a story like that is the guys would get a good laugh out of it. But the downside is what it could do to future P.I. business."

Her blood pounded, her face grew hot with humiliation. Her eyes flicked from the cops then back to him. He leaned back, eyebrows raised with a smirk crossing his face.

"How do I know you'll hold up your part of the bargain?"

"You're going to have to trust me. Just like I'm going to have to trust you're telling me the truth."

"What if there are other things I'd need in addition…"

"Like what?"

"You leave *me* out of this. You submit your evidence. You found it. You can use the story that *you* heard something in the field and figured someone was watching the house besides you."

"No can do. I'm not going to lie. What else?"

"You don't ask me who I'm working for."

"Agreed."

She peered down at the contents of the plastic bag, lifted her head and gazed at him. "If there is DNA on these cigarette butts and the perp is in the database, you may be the guy who busts the Rachel Mitchell investigation wide open. Of course, you're going to have to link the guy to the murder. From what I hear, they didn't find any DNA at the scene."

"It'd be a damn good start." He paused for a moment. "You saw him, didn't you? We need a good description."

"I didn't get a good look at him. He was about twenty feet from me when I noticed him. He wore a hooded, gray sweatshirt. He was watching the house with binoculars. I tried to take him from behind, but he knocked me down and I lost my gun. You know the rest."

"Think about it. Anything special about him?"

"You mean besides the fact he's got a hell of a right hook? No, not really. He's not much taller than me, has a wiry build, and he's Caucasian. Not much to go on. I don't think he was armed or he would have shot me. If you hadn't shown up, I would have followed him to his car to try to get a make, model and license number."

"Sorry I spoiled that for you. I probably saved your P.I. ass. It's not like he hasn't killed before." The thought of the perp hurting her any more than he had made Lane want to rip him apart.

"I'll be forever in your debt, Deputy Hansen," she fumed as she reached for her leather purse. "Thanks for the stimulating breakfast conversation. Too bad I have to go."

He grabbed her arm, pushing her back in her chair. "Where are you going to be if I have more questions?" He made no effort to remove his hand from her arm.

"Around." She pulled her arm out of his grip and said, "I suggest you keep your part of the bargain."

She pressed a twenty-dollar bill on the table, glared at him one more time, and then strode to the door. She couldn't get out of Mom's Diner fast enough.

Frankie sat across from Michael Brandt's desk, watching his face and waiting for an explosion, the seismic kind. She'd confessed, telling him the entire story with nothing left out. She was so nervous she abandoned her original plan of spinning the details. She'd always been a terrible liar.

"So Hansen has the cigarette butts and you gave him a description?" Michael asked.

"Yes, sir." She shifted a bit in her chair and cleared her throat.

"Good job."

"What did you say?" She couldn't have heard him correctly.

"Good job. Thanks to you, we're one step closer to nabbing this guy than we were yesterday this time."

"But he got away…"

"And you tried to stop him. Good job. We'll get him, Frankie. Don't be so hard on yourself."

She was still shaking her head in disbelief on how well the meeting went when she reached the sidewalk. She pulled out her cell to check for messages as she walked. One text message was from her partner, Ted. All was quiet at Golden Acres Farm. He'd slapped a GPS device on the frame beneath Anne's car so her movements could be tracked on their computers or cell phones. Mission accomplished.

She checked her watch. If she hurried, she had time to get some paperwork and calls done in her office before she started her shift at Golden Acres Farm. She turned the corner and noticed Deputy Lane Hansen leaning against the back of her red sports car.

"Ever heard of the stalking law, Deputy?"

"Nice car. P.I. business must be lucrative." He grinned, enjoying her annoyed expression.

"Why are you here?"

"I need for you to provide an official statement about what happened last night." He held up some paperwork between two fingers. He gave her one of his be-very-intimidated looks.

"If you think you're taking me to the station to fill out that form, you're badly mistaken. I'm busy. Damn it." His bossy attitude and glares were starting to piss her off. He needed to take her off his speed dial for threats and other miscellaneous crap. She crossed her arms over her breasts; her eyes glittered with annoyance.

"Calm down, Frankie. Isn't your office near here on Carrolton Street? We can go there." He watched her face as one eyebrow rose. He knew she was wondering how he knew where her office was. She didn't need to know about the report he'd had run on her.

She brushed past him and got in the car. The passenger door immediately flew open and Hansen got in. He jerked a lever to move the seat back as far as it would go to make room for his huge frame. "Thanks for the ride."

She rolled her eyes and shifted the gear to drive and headed toward her office. "Has anyone told you that you're very annoying?"

"Nope." Actually, his female cousins told him that all the time. Not that he planned to tell her.

"Let me be the first."

He checked her out while her attention was on the road. She rolled the windows down, letting fresh air wash through the car. The breeze picked up tendrils of her long, blonde hair pulling them out the window. She was definitely hot, and why hadn't he noticed her long legs before now? He liked her leopard heels. Suddenly he had a visual of making love with a naked Frankie wearing only the leopard heels. The resulting jolt of lust reminded him how long it had been since he'd been with a woman. Too damn long.

He put his arm across her seat, noting that she shifted uncomfortably as he ran his thumb down her neck. Something about him put her on edge. He thought about the kiss they'd shared the night before. She'd tasted as hot and sweet as she looked. He remembered how surprised he was when she kissed him back. Maybe that kiss was what made her so antsy around him. He hoped so.

Frankie pulled up to her building, jumped out of the car and went inside. He was on her heels right back to her office, ignoring her secretary who tried to get him to wait in reception. Yeah, right. He looked around her office. It was classy with padded leather chairs and a long glass desk with chrome legs. There was a window behind her desk, covered with wooden shutters. He leaned against a wall to look at several framed marksmanship medals and a couple of news articles about her business.

Ignoring him, Frankie pulled up her email on the computer and started scrolling through messages. He pushed the paperwork in front of her and refused to leave until she completed it.

Anne, Hank and Dan Wright stood on the front porch watching as the first escort car and semi-truck passed the house, carrying a huge blade needed to build one of eighty wind turbines on her twenty acres. It was more than 120 feet long and weighed seven tons. Dan estimated another semi with the second blade would be passing the house within the hour. Once all components arrived and were erected, each wind turbine would be around 300 feet tall. Anne thought of the first wind turbine she'd seen. It was a surreal steel monster with massive blades slicing the air in a serene, grassy hillside where a herd of cattle grazed.

Ink was dry on the contract and Hank's team had tilled the fields and built service roads that led to each plot of their new twenty acres wind farm. Soon they'd be generating energy.

"I'm going to head over to the site. I'm hoping that all of the components will arrive within the next few weeks and we can start construction. I'll keep you updated," said Dan. "Next time I see you both, I'll have a bottle of champagne with me so we can toast our new partnership."

After Dan left, Anne walked Hank to his truck and watched him toss his blue duffle bag in the back.

"I'll call you when I get to Jasper County."

"That'd be great."

"I hate to be away from Golden Acres right now."

"No worries. We're kicking off a new business and you're needed to learn as much as possible from the farmers who are already wind farming. We can learn from their successes and failures."

"Maybe I should postpone this trip considering everything that's going on."

"No, Hank. I need you to go. Things will be fine. I hired Deputy Hansen and I have my Glock."

He hesitated then climbed into the truck. "I'll call."

Anne went into the house and up to her study to work on her computer. She thought the house was too quiet without Daisy and Harley. She missed them but was glad they were safe away from the farm. She answered a few emails, ordered flowers to be sent to the Mitchell family, and worked for a couple of hours to put finishing touches on a software design.

It was mid-afternoon when she heard sirens cut through the quiet of the house like a knife. She moved to her bedroom window to see three deputy sheriff cars and an ambulance blaze past the house. A helicopter buzzed overhead. Her cell phone vibrated in her pocket.

"Anne, this is Dan."

"Hi, Dan. What's up?" She could hear a strain in his voice. Something was wrong.

"I think you might want to drive to the construction site. I'm here now."

"Is something wrong?"

"I had to call the sheriff, Anne. Please drive over here so I can talk to you in person."

She rushed to her car and raced down the road. By the time she reached the construction site, she noticed flashing lights atop the police and emergency vehicles and deputies setting up barricades to block the service road. She passed an officer carrying crime scene tape. She parked on the side of the road and searched on foot for Dan.

She saw him about twenty feet ahead, talking with the sheriff. He was pointing to something to his left. As she drew closer, he noticed her and moved toward her. Nervously, she ran her tongue across her dry lips. Icy fear twisted around her heart. Please God, no. “Please don’t let this be what I think it is,” she prayed.

When Dan reached her, he clutched Anne’s arms to stop her from going closer. He used his body to block her vision of the area near the sheriff.

Her eyes were wide and watery as she searched his face. She feared what he would say. She began to shake as fearful images formed in her mind.

“Anne, let’s walk back to your car to talk.”

“No. Tell me here and now.” She gazed at Dan. His facial muscles were strained and he looked as if he were afraid to tell her what he needed to say. His fingers still clutched her arms and had tightened so much they started to hurt.

“Anne, we found…”

They turned to see a silver truck careening down the road, wheels spitting gravel, creating huge clouds of dust. Several deputies shouted and waved their arms, directing the driver to stop. The truck skidded to a stop. A man jumped out, pushed past the deputies, and ran toward Dan and Anne, calling her name. Michael?

She stared at him, not noticing the tears streaming down her face. No. She shook her head. No, this cannot be happening again. No. This was a nightmare and she would wake up soon. She started feeling nauseous, then everything began swirling around her. She felt the blackness closing in and fell to the ground.

The rocking back and forth was soothing and she imagined being held in her grandmother’s arms as a child. Why was there so much pain in her head? The rocking felt so good; surely it would make the pain go away. Something cool touched her forehead. Someone called her name. Grandma? She felt wet tears sliding out of her eyes and down her cheeks. Why was she crying? Why was she shivering? Her eyes were so heavy, but she had to open them to see who was calling her name.

When she was finally able to open her eyes, everything was spinning and it was hard to focus.

“Anne?” His voice was low and filled with concern.

“Michael? You’re not supposed to be here,” she whispered.

He laughed softly with relief and pulled her closer. She was conscious. He rocked her gently back and forth on the sofa, planting soft kisses on her hair and face. "Are you okay, honey?"

She gazed at him, wanting to put all the pieces together so that they made sense. Why did he look so worried?

"What happened? Where am I?"

"You passed out and now you're home." He scanned her face and saw the same wild look in her eyes he'd seen after the carjacking. She was in shock.

"No. I don't faint. Never have."

He noticed she was shivering again, so he covered her with a soft throw he found tossed across the arm of the sofa. He glanced at the fire dying down to embers in the fireplace and made a mental note to get more firewood when he could.

"Where's Dan? He wants to tell me something."

"It can wait."

"Dan called me," she remembered, the haze in her head clearing. "He asked me to come to the construction site. Something happened. Something bad."

"Honey, it can wait. Let's get you checked out by a doctor."

"No. I don't need a doctor. I feel better. Let me sit up."

His phone vibrated and Michael pulled it out of his jacket pocket.

"Brandt. Just a second." He turned to Anne. "I need to take this. Are you going to be okay?"

"Yes, of course."

He stood, stared down at her for a moment, and then walked into the dining room. He was talking softly and she strained to listen.

"Don't worry about the search warrant. I caught Judge Anderson at the courthouse and he's already signed it. Go ahead and send the Crime Scene Techs in."

Search warrant? Crime Scene Techs? It had happened again. This wasn't a nightmare. It was real. Another body had been found on her land and it was her fault. He was sending a message to *her*. Another gift? Another victim?

She knew with chilling and absolute certainty she was next.

Three deputy cars passed Frankie near the farm when she arrived to relieve Ted, and she realized shit had hit the fan. She saw flashing lights in the distance and aimed her car toward them. She passed Anne's house, noticed Michael's truck, but did not see Hansen's. She continued until she reached a deputy standing next to a barricade that crossed the road. In the distance, there were flashing lights and people scurrying about. The deputy moved toward her car.

"Ma'am, I'm sorry, but I'm going to have to ask you to turn around. You can't go beyond this point."

Frankie eyed the young deputy thoughtfully, and then climbed out of her car, fully aware he was checking her out. She was wearing a tight turtleneck with black jeans and the leopard print pumps. Her work clothes were still in her trunk. Pulling a tube of red gloss from her purse, she ran it across her lips.

"I don't think we've met, deputy," she purred. "My name is Frankie Hansen. You may know my brother, Lane." She beamed her most dazzling smile at him.

"I didn't know Lane had a sister."

"He does and I'm her. I'm studying at the police academy so I can be a deputy someday like Lane."

"That's great. My name is Ed Smith."

"Good to meet you, Ed. I heard what happened. When did it go down?"

"The body was found around 3:00 o'clock. We were called shortly after. Crime scene techs are in there now."

"Know who it is?"

"Just know it's another young female like the last one. They just took her to the coroner."

"Thanks, Ed." She got back in her car, threw the gear in reverse and turned around. Holy shit. Another murder? Another body found on Golden Acres Farm. Anne Mason must be freaking out.

She slowed down when she reached Anne's house and gazed down the long lane. Lane Hansen's truck was now in the driveway and he was standing on the porch talking with Michael. She drove ahead to hide her car in the wooded area near the cornfield. She opened the trunk, pulled on a black thermal hoodie and camouflage pants. She tossed her pumps in the trunk and put on a pair of socks, then her boots. Unzipping her backpack, she pulled out her Glock 23, .45 caliber automatic hand gun. She tossed in an extra magazine and tucked the gun in her holster. She threw the backpack over her shoulder, slammed the trunk, and then entered the field.

Frankie crept slowly through the corn row, consistently looking in each direction to see if she had company again tonight. She was ready for him and was up for kicking some sick killer ass. She'd have no problem shooting him, either. She did a belly crawl until she reached a spot where she pulled out her binoculars. An ambulance was parked in the drive now. Michael Brandt was on the porch talking with a couple of EMTs who looked like they were ready to leave. When they boarded the ambulance, she pulled out her cell phone.

"Michael, this is Frankie. What's going on?"

"Where are you?"

"Field."

"You know about the body?"

"Yes, sir. How is Ms. Mason?"

"She's better. I just had her looked over by a couple of EMTs."

"Any new instructions for me?"

"No, just keep your eyes peeled tonight. This sick fuck is going to try to get to her. It may not be tonight. There's too much activity. But soon."

"Yes, sir."

She tucked the cell phone in the backpack and focused her binoculars on the house. She saw Hansen doing a survey of the perimeter, pausing to check windows and doors as he went. She pulled a ham sandwich and a can of Red Bull out of her bag. It was going to be a long night.

In the kitchen, Anne poured hot water into a mug then dunked a chamomile tea bag. She stirred with a spoon until the liquid darkened, added a dollop of honey, and then tossed the bag in the waste can. She picked up the mug, walked to the living room and sat next to the fireplace to watch the fire Michael had built. She watched flames licking the logs in red, yellow and blue flickering hues. Michael was on the porch talking on his cell phone. She didn't look forward to yet another difficult conversation they would have when he came in.

She wondered how and when the killer would contact her. Would he send another note? Would he call her? Would he break into her house to get to her?

Michael had told her the body was a young female. Her mind went to the dead girl's family who were about to experience the anguish that accompanies losing a loved one who died too young in such a violent way. Shivering, she wrapped her arms around herself and moved closer to the fire for warmth.

She heard the front door open and watched Michael come in with an armful of firewood. He placed it in the wood tray near the fireplace. Poking at the fire a bit, he added a log and then gazed at her. She hated that he was looking at her with such concern in his eyes.

"Are you okay?"

"Yes. Please stop asking me."

"Okay."

"You look tired, Michael. You should go home soon." His expression darkened, just as she knew it would. He was just as stubborn as she was. If the situation were reversed, she would probably behave the same way. But she'd make him leave anyway.

"I'm not tired. In fact, I'm thinking about getting my briefcase out of my truck and tackle the stack of work in there. Is it okay if I use your computer again?"

"Nice try. You're not staying. There is a deputy parked outside. All the windows and doors are locked. I'm fine."

"I'm staying."

"Michael, we've already discussed this."

"No, *you* discussed it."

"How badly do you want this killer to be prosecuted to the fullest extent of the law so that he can never hurt another human being?"

"I think you know how much. I'd like to tear him apart with my bare hands."

"Then we agree. You can't stay here with me. You cannot risk being accused by some defense attorney of letting your personal relationships impact your professional judgment."

"Anne..."

"A lot of people are counting on you to put this guy away—including me."

"Will you promise to call me if you need me?"

"I promise."

"There's something I need to do before I go." He went to his truck, and returned holding an electric drill and something in a brown paper bag. He pulled a deadbolt lock out of the bag and then proceeded to install it on the front door.

Frankie pulled the hood up to cover her head and watched Michael's truck lights as they disappeared into the night. She was still curious about what he had going with Anne Mason, but it was none of her business. She needed to drop it.

The wind was picking up and she could feel the temperature dropping as the TV weather guy said it would. She was glad she'd packed an extra thermos of espresso. Thank goodness for Starbucks.

She stiffened when she heard movement in the field. She focused her binoculars to the left then the right. Nothing.

She focused back on the house. Anne's bedroom light was the only one on now. The moon moved behind a cloud so the yard was dark and hard to see, even with her binoculars. Frankie decided to switch to her brand-new night-vision pair soon. She'd splurged on a pair of waterproof and fog-proof night-vision binoculars with a 200-yard detection range last Christmas. It was her yearly holiday gift to herself and tonight would be her first chance to use them.

She was digging in her backpack to find them when a very large man dropped down in the corn row next to her and soundly popped her on the butt. She immediately reached for her gun, but his hand clamped down on hers, squeezing tight.

"Are you out here studying the stars again?" Deputy Lane

Hansen's smile stretched across his face. He was proud of himself. He hadn't done a stealthy Army crawl in quite a while and this one was definitely a success. She had no clue he'd been watching her for fifteen minutes before he made his move. She almost jumped out of her skin when he landed beside her.

"You touch my butt again and *you're* going to be the one seeing stars."

"You pose as my sister again and you're going to get more than a pop on the butt. What did you say to Ed? He asked me for your number."

She shrugged and met his glare with her best have-no-clue-what-you're-talking-about look.

"Aren't you supposed to be doing surveillance closer to the house? Doing it at your truck up near the barn sounds like a good idea."

"Why? I just walked the perimeter. I don't want the perp to see me in the truck and get scared off. I want him to get brave and try something so I can catch his ass."

"Well, that's something we can agree on."

"What's in backpack?"

"Just some P.I. tools and some personal girly stuff. Nothing you'd be interested in." She shoved it a little farther away from his reach, hoping he would be put off by the mention of girly stuff.

He reached across her to grab the backpack, his hard body pinning her to the ground. She wiggled to get him off but he just laughed until he was able to pull the bag across her back. He unzipped it and rummaged around while dodging her attempts to grab it back. He pulled out a thermos.

"What's in here?" He twisted off the top, found two plastic cups in the bag, and then poured some steamy brew in both. He handed a cup to her, and then swallowed a mouthful. "Excellent. It's Espresso. You've got good taste, Frankie. Starbucks? Double shot?"

Trying to ignore him, she sipped the Starbucks Espresso with a double shot as she focused her binoculars on the house. Deputy Lane Hansen had to be the most infuriating man in the world, possibly the universe. In no time, she heard him digging around in the backpack again.

"Oh, these are *sweet*."

She turned to see him holding her brand-new waterproof and fog-proof night-vision binoculars with 200-yard detection range up to his eyes. Damn it.

"Can you be any more freaking annoying?"

"You kissed me back last night." He put the binoculars down for a moment to gaze at her.

"No, I didn't. Don't be ridiculous." It was a lie, but she could tell he wasn't as certain that she kissed him back as he was trying to sound.

"You just keep telling yourself that." He smirked then went back to the binoculars.

Suddenly, he bopped her on the arm. "Holy shit. Look at the back door. Do you see what I see?"

"Goddamn it. He's working on the lock. Run!"

She jumped to her feet and ran at full sprint, her feet kicking up clods of dirt in the field as she went. Hansen passed her once they hit the front yard and raced to the back.

By the time she reached the back door, it was wide open and Hansen was somewhere inside. The back porch light was broken, the fragments of glass crunching under her boots as she moved forward. She pulled out a small flashlight along with her Glock. She held the gun in her right hand, the flashlight in her left making a V with her arms. Inside the kitchen, she moved the flashlight back and forth. Clear. She was almost to the front of the house, when she heard a scuffle upstairs. Damn. Anne's bedroom was upstairs.

"Hansen? Where are you?" No response. Still holding the flashlight and gun in position, she slowly crept up the stairs. Once she reached the top, she saw Hansen lying on the floor in the hallway. She ran to him, running the flashlight over him checking for injuries.

"Hey, Hansen. Talk to me." He lay motionless. She reached for his wrist and could feel a pulse. She moved the flashlight up and down his body again. It was then she noticed several circular marks on his neck. Shit. The perp has a stun gun. Hansen lay unable to move, his muscles jerking and disabled from the shock.

She heard the back door slam and raced down the back stairs, taking them two at a time until she reached the kitchen. She rushed out the back door and could see the perp running in the distance.

"Stop!" she screamed. She lifted her arms, aimed and shot above his head. He kept running.

She hurried after him. If she couldn't catch up with him, he'd reach the cornfield and she would lose him. He was almost there. Too late. She watched him disappear into the field.

She returned to the house. Where was Anne Mason? She crept back up the stairs. There was a light shining beneath the door of the first room. She twisted the door knob. It was locked.

"Anne, are you in there?" She waited a few seconds, but there was no answer.

"Anne, I'm here to help you. I need you to slowly open your door and let me see you're all right." She kept her gun and flashlight pointed at the door. She could not be certain who was inside. "Anne, can you hear me?"

She looked down the hall. Hansen was sitting up now and cursing. She looked at the door again. "Anne, you're safe. I'm here to help you. I am going to open your door now. I need to see that you are okay." She leaned in to listen. There were still no sounds coming from the room.

"Anne, please unlock the door. I'm here to help you."

Click.

Slowly Frankie twisted the doorknob, then pushed on the door until she could see Anne standing next to her bed, holding what looked to be a pink Glock that was aimed at her chest.

"Anne, my name is Frankie. You can trust me. I need you to lay your gun on the bed." She used her calmest voice although her heart was in her throat. Fear made people do stupid things with guns.

"He was here, wasn't he? He's going to kill me. Where is he now?" Her eyes were wide but her expression was now more anger than fear.

"Anne, he got away. Did you hear the gunshot? That was me. But he got away. You don't need your gun now. Please lay it on the bed."

"Who are you?" Anne searched Frankie's face, still holding onto the gun.

"I am a deputy with the Sheriff's Department," she lied. "I

need for you to lay down your gun so I can help my partner. He's injured."

Anne nodded and placed the gun on her bed and Frankie raced to Hansen's side.

"Do you want me to help you stand up?" She reached for his arm but he pushed her away.

"No." He pulled himself up and leaned on the wall. Waves of exhaustion hit him. He began to rub the muscles in his arms and legs. "That prick is going down."

"Should I call for an ambulance?" With cell phone in hand, Anne watched them from the doorframe of her room.

"Hansen, give me your wrist so I can take your pulse."

He leaned down next to her ear and whispered. "Are you trying to play doctor with me?" He rested his hand on the small of her back.

Frankie glared up him, and then noticed Anne watching them at the other end of the hall. She raised her voice so Anne would hear. "Deputy Hansen, it looks like you're going to be all right." She gently pushed him away.

"Anne, I need for you to go back in your bedroom and lock the door while I check the downstairs. Deputy Hansen will be right here and I'll be right back."

With gun in hand, she headed down the front stairs and checked each room until she reached the kitchen. She pulled the back door closed and checked the lock. It was still operational. The perp probably used a credit card to open it. She was on her way back upstairs to talk to Anne when she noticed the white envelope in the middle of the kitchen table with Anne's name written in large block letters. She froze.

Chapter 9

"Don't touch it!"

Startled, Frankie whirled around to see Anne Mason and Deputy Hansen in the doorframe. She watched Anne move to a kitchen drawer to pull out a plastic bag and a pair of latex gloves. She slipped the gloves over her hands and lifted the flap of the envelope. She retrieved the folded paper inside and laid it flat on the table.

If you think I can't get to you, think again.

There's nothing that will stop me from getting to you. Nothing, bitch.

I'm looking forward to savoring the moment you breathe your last.

You won't get away from me again. We'll have our private party.

By the way, what did you think of my latest gift?

Anne read the note again, fear and anger knotting inside her. Getting away *again*? *Private party*? Weren't those the words her carjacker used in August? Christ. Had he been trying to get to her since August? Had he followed her here? The thought tore at her insides.

She slipped the note back into the envelope then inserted it into the plastic bag and placed it back on the table. She pushed past Hansen and climbed the stairs up to her room. She needed a new plan and she needed one fast.

Frankie watched Hansen pull a cell phone out of his pocket

and push some buttons. He moved toward the front porch and she called after him. "Are you calling this in?"

When he nodded, she pulled out her own cell phone, rushed out the back door and headed for the field to collect her things. She had her own call to make and that was to Michael Brandt.

By the time Michael reached the house, five deputy cars and the crime scene investigation van were parked in the drive. Flashing lights danced on the front lawn and house.

He joined Deputy Hansen and Sheriff Miller who stood on the front porch talking. Crime scene tape lined the railings of the porch and rustled in the wind. He could hear a buzz of activity within the house. Where was Anne?

"Just tell me everything you remember about what happened." Sheriff Miller pulled a pen and a small pad of paper out of his pocket and prepared to write.

"I didn't see him in the upstairs hallway. He jumped me with a stun gun and got away." Hansen ran his fingers through his hair. Christ, he was an idiot. How the hell did this happen? His chances at that detective promotion were blown for sure—high test score or not.

"What did he look like?" Sheriff Miller glanced at Michael then returned to Hansen.

"I know he was wearing a ski mask, but it happened so fast, I can't tell you what else. Wait a minute. He was wearing gloves."

Michael glared at the deputy. Exactly how does a perp get past an armed deputy *and* a P.I., jimmy the back door open, then overpower the deputy, who is the size of a barn, with a damn stun gun, then avoid getting shot by an Army trained sharpshooter? He shook his head in disgust. He wanted to hit something or someone.

He was angry but also felt an overpowering sense of guilt that he hadn't taken the time to install a deadbolt lock on the back door along with the front. He shared part of the blame for this fiasco. And what in the hell was taking so long for the security equipment to be installed? He made a mental note to ream Rick Davies.

"This perp's got balls coming back here after what happened

last night." Sheriff Miller chomped on a piece of gum as he closed the note pad and pushed it in his pants pocket.

"He probably noticed the lack of law enforcement at the house," Michael said, and it came out as an accusation.

"You can keep your damn finger-pointing to yourself." Sheriff Miller's reaction was explosive and swift; his eyes bulged and his frown deepened.

Michael ignored his outburst and watched as eight or nine deputies armed with flashlights entered the cornfield. Frankie should be long gone by now. He'd sent her home for the rest of the night.

"What are they doing?" He asked.

"They're doing a grid search. We might get lucky and find he's still out there. If not, he may have dropped something that could lead us to him." Hansen answered.

Michael nodded and noticed the sheriff was still glaring at him.

"What are *you* doing here anyway?" The sheriff eyed him suspiciously. "You're not a cop anymore, Brandt. You need to back off and leave this investigation to the investigators. We'll bring you what you need to prosecute."

"I'm here in case any additional warrants are needed," he lied. It was none of Sheriff Miller's business that he was here to see Anne. He scowled at him then eyed the crime scene tape on the front door. "Can I go inside?"

"No. The crime scene techs are dusting for fingerprints in the hallway on the second floor and the back door. Doubt if they find anything though since the bastard was wearing gloves. At any rate, they don't want you or anyone else tramping around in their crime scene corrupting evidence."

Michael stepped off the porch before he lost his temper and punched an armed law enforcement officer. He got in his truck and pretended to be looking for something in the glove box.

"Come on Hansen, let's go interview our witness." Sheriff Miller and Hansen headed to the back of the house and entered through the kitchen door. Michael was close behind.

The two were met by a crime scene technician who announced they were finished and were heading back.

A second crime scene tech was holding out his mug as Anne filled it with hot coffee. He took a sip and watched her dump more coffee in the coffee maker and flip the switch.

It was going to be a long night and she was bone-tired. She was also sick of the commotion and take-over of her home that was now outlined with crime scene tape. What happened to the home that was to be her oasis? It seemed like a long, long time ago when she'd packed up her things and moved to the country for some privacy, peace and quiet. Things certainly hadn't turned out how she planned.

She pulled coffee mugs out for the sheriff and Deputy Hansen from the cabinet. She'd seen Michael's truck in the driveway and wondered where he was.

"Did you guys get any prints?"

"We got some, but they may not belong to the perp. We'll let you know."

The crime scene tech scanned the room, noticed the note in plastic and leaned across the kitchen table to retrieve it.

"Hey, let me copy the note before you take it." Hansen pulled out his pad and pen out of his pocket and started writing.

When he finished, he handed the note to the crime tech who tucked it in his bag along with his camera then headed for their van.

"Let's talk about the note, Ms. Mason. We could use your take on it." Sheriff Miller watched her as she slid a mug of hot coffee to him then to Hansen.

"I know who wrote the note," she said, noting their surprised expressions.

"Are you saying you know who the perp is?" Hansen asked.

"I think the same man who carjacked me in August wrote the note."

"Why do you think that?"

"Read the fourth line of the note. He says I won't get away from him *again.* That refers to the night he carjacked my car. He told me that night he had a *'private party'* planned for the two of us. He would have killed me in August had I not driven into a tree."

"If you're right, we're talking about a guy with some long-term anger. Who do you know that would be that pissed off at you?" Sheriff Miller focused his usual scowl at her.

"I can't think of anyone." She shrugged her shoulders. Who would be so angry with her that he would want her dead?

"I can. Your ex had to be furious when you got the farm he thought he was going to inherit," replied the sheriff.

"I paid Allan $500,000 when I sold the house and my shares in my computer company. He never wanted the farm. He wanted cash."

"We checked on Allan. He's living in Las Vegas. But that doesn't mean he isn't involved."

"Allan is not a murderer. Anyway, the carjacker didn't sound like Allan. I would have known his voice."

"One thing I've learned in thirty years of law enforcement is that you can't predict what others will do." Sheriff Miller took a gulp of his coffee. "Allan Long is still not off my radar. He could have hired someone to do this."

"It's not Allan."

"Okay, if it's not Allan, who is it? You have to know this guy. Who would want to hurt you?"

Before she could answer, the sheriff's cell phone buzzed and he went into the hallway to take the call. He returned a short time later.

"I'm sorry, Ms. Mason. Hansen and I need to go. The doc is ready to start the autopsy."

"Is the autopsy for the body found near my wind turbine construction site?"

"Yes."

"Who is it?" Anne cringed as she asked the question. Whoever it was, it was her fault. The sick bastard was leaving these bodies for her as a reminder that her turn would come soon.

"Sorry, I can't share information about an active investigation."

He chugged the rest of his coffee then set the empty mug in the sink. "I'm going to add another deputy to watch your house for the day shift. Hansen can continue surveillance at night. He'll be back later."

"Thank you." Anne's expression was filled with wariness.

Does this offer mean he's changed his mind about her being a suspect? Does it mean he believes her?

"I'll give you a call later." With that he and Hansen headed for their cars out the front door.

Moments later, Michael entered the kitchen from the back door and pulled Anne into his arms.

"You shouldn't be here," she whispered. She hoped she sounded firm because she wasn't at all sure she was strong enough to send him away tonight.

He covered her mouth with his own to smother her words, and crushed her against him. All Michael could think about was how grateful he was that she was alive and in his arms. He kissed the top of her head and wondered how much more she could take. This is why he'd planned a distraction.

"When was the last time you ate anything?" He tucked a strand of hair behind her ear, as he looked down at her.

"I can't remember."

"Let's do a junk food run."

"Seriously? Now?"

"Dead serious. How does a breaded tenderloin sandwich with mayo, tomato and lettuce sound?"

"It sounds good, but I don't think I should leave the house."

"Steak fries?"

"We really shouldn't be seen together."

"How about fried green tomatoes instead of the fries? And add Ben and Jerry's Red Velvet Cake ice cream for dessert?"

"Who's driving?"

Michael smiled, pulled out his keys, grabbed her hand, then led her outside toward his truck. Once inside, she pulled down the mirror on the visor and decided she needed a serious makeover. God, she looked like crap. Could she look any more tired and tense? She pulled a lip gloss tube out of her pocket and coated her lips.

She glanced at Michael. Could this man be any better looking? She wondered what he saw in her. She'd had one problem after the other since the day they met. Surely, he could find a woman who didn't have a psycho killer stalking her.

"It's almost midnight. Do you think we'll find a place open?"

"I'm sure of it."

Fifteen minutes later they pulled into the empty parking lot of Sarah's Home Cooking restaurant.

"Darn it. It's closed."

Michael jumped out and eased around the truck to open the passenger door.

"It's open." He smiled and helped her out of the truck.

A silver-haired lady wearing a wide smile and an apron came to the door, unlocked it, and turned on the outside light for them. She ushered them in, locked the door and threw her arms around Michael.

"It was so good to get your call. It's been too long." She planted a big kiss on Michael's cheek before she turned to Anne. "So you're Michael's young lady."

"Anne, this is Sarah," said Michael.

"It's nice to meet you, Sarah. But isn't your restaurant closed?"

"Not for my Michael. I have a table ready for you by the fireplace. I thought you might like that." She led them to a round table dressed with a white tablecloth, then headed toward the kitchen.

"So we have the place to ourselves?" asked Anne. She looked around the room then leaned back in her chair to gaze at the large red-brick fireplace where several logs burned.

"Sarah is an old friend of my parents." Michael gazed at Anne, then covered her hand with his, intertwining their fingers.

"Where are your parents?" Anne realized there was much she didn't know about Michael.

"They're living it up in Orlando. They moved there a couple of years ago after Dad retired."

"Are you close to them?"

"I guess so. They call me every Sunday. I don't visit them as much as I should. What about your parents?"

"They died a few years ago in a car accident. We weren't close. My grandmother raised me."

Sarah appeared holding two platters with tenderloin sandwiches, steak fries, fried green tomatoes, ranch dressing and salads. She poured root beer into icy mugs. "Would you two like anything else?"

"Sarah, you're amazing. Thank you for doing this."

Sarah hugged Michael again, squeezed Anne's arm and disappeared.

"Oh my God," Anne sighed as she took her first bite of the sandwich. "This is incredible." She snagged a couple of fried green tomatoes then covered them with ranch dressing.

They chowed down, eating in silence until Sarah returned for the dishes.

"I undoubtedly gained ten pounds with that meal," Anne complained.

"You could use ten extra pounds," said Michael.

"Oh, please. Ten more pounds and I move right into sizes carried only by Tent and Awning."

"If there is one thing I don't understand, it's the way women perceive their bodies. You all think you're fat. I bet *you've* been on at least two diets in the past six months."

"You'd lose." Actually, she'd been on three different diets but she wouldn't be telling him that.

"I like your curves, Anne." He did an appreciative scan of her body with his eyes. "I like them a lot."

A sensuous light passed between them and her cheeks burned in remembrance of his hand sliding over her hip after they'd made love.

Sarah appeared, "Would you like your ice cream now?"

Anne shook her head. "Sarah, that was the best meal I've had in a long, long time. Thank you so much." She stood to hug the older woman.

"We'll take that to go, so you can lock up. Thanks again for doing this." He slipped a hundred-dollar bill in her apron pocket when she brought out the ice cream in a white paper bag and hugged them both at the door.

"Please come back. Michael, tell your folks I said hello."

Michael helped Anne get in his truck, then moved to the driver's side and slid behind the wheel. Soon they were headed back to her house.

"Tell me about the note." He gazed at her and hated the way she tensed when he mentioned the note, but this was a discussion he wouldn't let her avoid.

"Not much to tell." She avoided his eyes and focused on the road.

She could feel him staring a hole in her.

"What?" she asked.

"Why aren't you telling me what was in the note?"

"For the same reason you didn't tell me the whole story when I asked you about the conversation you had with the sheriff in my kitchen," she hissed. Who was he to question her when he gave her zip when it came to the sheriff prying about his relationship with her? Her temper flared and she glared at him with burning, reproachful eyes.

"Whoa. Where did that anger come from?"

"I'm not telling you about the note because you'll go into protection overload."

"You're damn right. By the way, I was on the back porch and heard everything you said to the sheriff. That note changes everything."

"How?"

"You know how. This guy has been after you since August. He's the same prick who carjacked you. He's already tried to kill you once."

"That's my problem, not yours." She shot him fierce glare.

Furious, he punched the brakes and parked the truck at the side of the road. He shoved the gear into park. "You did *not* just say that."

"I mean it. You can't keep taking on my problems." Especially when taking on her problems put his life at risk.

"And *you* can't keep making decisions for *me*! Like the one you made about me staying away from you. I had no vote or even discussion on that one, and I haven't slept a full night since." His face was a glowering mask of rage. He put the truck in drive and headed to her house.

They spent the rest of the drive in silence. When he pulled in the driveway and parked, he grabbed her arm so she couldn't jump out of the truck.

"Let go."

"I'm sorry I got so angry." He loosened his grip on her arm and kissed her on the cheek. "Honey, we need to talk."

She looked down at her hands. "Talk about what?"

"Your safety. I want you to move in with me. Your house is not safe. He wouldn't have been able to get in if it was."

"No, I'm *not* moving in with you." He couldn't be serious. Talk about a conflict in interest. There has to be something in the attorney good ethics book about moving your witness in with you. Besides, he hadn't even told her he was in love with her, let alone make the kind of a commitment that moving in together represents.

"Yes, you are."

"No, I'm *not*." She lifted the handle and jumped out of the truck. By the time she got to his side, he was out and glaring at her.

"Wait a minute." He got back in the truck, took his handgun out of the glove box and slipped it in the waist of his jeans. When he got out, he clutched her hand. "I'm taking you in and checking things out."

"Okay, Michael." She saw the determination in his eyes and knew a losing battle when she saw one. He could check the house. Then he could leave.

At the front door, she handed him the keys and watched him unlock the door.

"Would you please stay here until I get back?" He said as they moved inside. He turned and locked the door then began checking each room on the first floor. He returned a few minutes later and passed her on his way up the stairs. She stood exactly where he left her by the front door.

She listened as he checked each room upstairs. She watched him as he came down the stairs, placing his gun in the back of his jeans. He had an odd gleam in his eyes as he stared at her.

"All clear, right?"

He didn't answer. Instead he backed her against the door and kissed her with such intensity it made her heart hammer against her ribs as explosive currents surged through her. She should be pushing against his chest to stop him, but she was pulling him closer so she could feel his hard length pressed against her. And she was kissing him right back. She tightened her arms around his neck.

He swept her into his arms and climbed the stairs until they reached her bedroom. She held on tight, covering his neck and face with gentle kisses. He kicked her door closed and locked it as she nibbled his ear lobe. When he put her on the floor, she struggled with his leather jacket until he took it off and threw it on the love seat. She pulled on his shirt until he lifted it over his shoulders. She ran her fingers over his pecs, loving the hard smoothness of his muscular body.

He backed her closer to the bed and placed his gun, cell phone and wallet on a small table. Then he pulled her back into his arms and hungrily reclaimed her mouth. His tongue sent shivers of desire racing through her.

He tugged her denim jacket from her shoulders and sent it flying. He lifted her shirt over her shoulders and then unbuttoned her jeans and pulled the zipper down. She sat on the bed to remove her Reeboks, then shoved her jeans to the floor with her foot. Her bra was the next to go, then her panties.

Not taking his eyes off her for a second, he pulled off his boots, and eased her back on the bed. He lay on his side, balanced on one arm as he ran his fingers around the curve of her breasts, down to her belly button, then down more until he was cupping her.

"Oh, my God." A sharp burst of bliss flooded through her as she arched, wanting him never to stop.

His mouth moved over her breasts, his tongue tantalizing the buds which had swollen to their fullest.

God, she wanted *this* man. She wrapped her arms around his neck and pulled him into a kiss, then another. She wasn't satisfied until she felt the full length of him crushing her body to the bed. She arched against him again and again, showing him the tempo to bind their bodies together. She felt the roughness of his jeans rub against her and realized he was still wearing them. Her fingers raced to unbutton the fly and pull on the zipper. He got up and shoved his jeans to the floor. He reached for his wallet and she heard the wrapper rip before he covered himself.

He returned to her, covering her with the wonderful weight of his body. She arched her hips up to meet him as he pushed inside her. She gasped at the force of it and wrapped her legs around him. Her body melted against his, filled with him as he thrust again and again, until he shattered her world into a million glowing stars.

The soft chiming of Michael's cell phone alarm woke her. He reached across her, grabbed the phone to turn off the alarm, then kissed her. She sighed, pulled his leg across her hip and cuddled closer to him.

"Can't we sleep a little longer?" She pressed against him, enjoying the warmth of his hard body.

He stroked her hair and watched her face. He wondered if he should tell her that he loved her. A part of him thought she might bolt at the mention of the "L" word. Another part of him didn't know if he could take it if she didn't love him back. He had never felt this close to anyone. It was frightening new territory.

"Hey, *you* aren't sleeping." Her blue eyes looked up at him, searching his face. Her finger rubbed against his lower lip, before she kissed him. "You know, I am suddenly not feeling so sleepy." She slowly stroked her fingers down his neck, through the ridge that divided his chest, and down lower until he groaned and pulled her into a deep kiss. She pulled him atop her, reveling in the heat and weight of his body.

Later, she stood in the bathroom brushing her teeth, watching in the mirror as Michael got out of the shower. The man was ripped. He grabbed a towel and snapped it at her. "Are you checking me out again?"

She laughed and watched him move to the bedroom to get dressed. She liked how at ease he was with his body. He thought nothing about walking around her bedroom completely nude. She thought of making love with him last night and again this morning, then showering with him. A surge of heat shot through her body. She already wanted him again.

"A deputy just arrived. Looks like the sheriff kept his word." He watched at the window, and then turned to her. "I have to go to the office for a couple of hours." He walked to where she stood in the bathroom, tugged at the belt to her robe until it opened and pulled her close to him. His hands moved under the robe to caress her bare skin as he kissed her.

"What time will you be back?" she asked.

"No later than two o'clock." He kissed her another time, and then headed down the stairs. She heard the front door close and the sound of his truck's engine as it roared to life. She went to the window to watch his truck until it disappeared at the end of the driveway.

She closed her eyes for a moment. She knew what she had to do. She couldn't continue putting all the people she cared about at risk—Daisy, Hank, Michael. *She* was responsible for the killer's wrath. They were innocents in a truly fucked-up situation beyond anyone's control. But there was something *she* could do to protect them. It was time for a new plan. She walked across the room to her closet and pulled out a suitcase. She picked up her cell phone on the bedside table and called Hank.

It was mid-afternoon and Frankie was loading groceries into the trunk of her car when her cell phone buzzed. She glanced at the display before putting it to her ear.

"Hey, Michael." She closed the trunk and got into her car.

"Where is she?" Even though he told himself to dial it down a notch, he found himself shouting into the phone.

"What are you talking about?"

"Where is Anne Mason?" Michael sounded both freaked out and furious.

"We put a GPS on her SUV. Wait just a second and I'll pull it up on my cell phone."

"I'm looking at her goddamn SUV. Where is she?"

Shit. Wasn't Ted watching the house? "Let me check some things and I'll call you back." She selected Ted's number on her cell and tapped her fingers nervously on the steering wheel until he answered.

"Ted, where are you?"

"I'm in the field watching the house."

"Have you seen Anne Mason?"

"No. There hasn't been much activity today. There's a deputy outside the house now. That's a first. He just did a perimeter check. Hank and a field hand left a couple of hours ago in his truck. The rest of the field hands are out in the field. You know, the usual."

"Give me a description of the field hand you saw with Hank."

"He looked to be about 5 foot 10 inches and kind of skinny for a guy. He was wearing a denim barn jacket and a black baseball cap. He came out of the house with Hank."

"Did you see this field hand go *into* the house?"

"Come to think of it, I didn't."

"Shit. We've lost her."

She disconnected the call then called Michael, bracing herself for the rage he'd fire in her direction.

"She's gone."

"No shit, Sherlock. How did she get away?"

"I think she dressed like a farm hand and left with Hank."

Michael walked to Anne's closet to look inside. He noticed there were gaps between some of the hangers. Some of her clothes were missing.

"Damn it. Where'd she go? It's dangerous for her to be out there. The killer is watching her."

"Ted is on his way to the airport with her photo to work his charm on the airline agents. If she flew somewhere, he'll find out where. I'll call the rental car services. We'll find her, Michael."

"Call me as soon as you find out anything." He was pissed. He was also scared. What if the perp followed her? She needed protection, whether she wanted it or not.

His cell phone buzzed almost the instant he disconnected the call to Frankie.

"Michael Brandt."

"Michael, this is Doc Meade. I thought you might want to hear some of the autopsy results."

"What did you find?"

"The victim died the same way Rachel Mitchell died, from strangulation. He used his hands again."

"Was the rest of the M.O. the same?"

"Yes, the body was nude and he'd washed her down with bleach just like the other one."

"What about the ribbon?"

"Yes, this time the ribbon was pink. The Crime Scene Techs are processing it now for prints. Unless he slipped up, he used gloves like last time."

"Were you able to come up with an identification?"

"Yes, our victim is Cindy Barrett. She was a thirty-year-old high school teacher in Fountain County. She's been missing for a month. We had her dental records."

"Thanks, Doc."

Michael shook his head with disgust. Questions swirled in his head like a tornado. How could anyone hurt an innocent woman like that? How could anyone take her life? And where in the hell was Anne? What would he do if the perp reached her before he did?

He heard some commotion outside, so he moved to a window where he saw several news media vans approaching the house. He watched as the deputy ran toward them, waving his arms, motioning for them to get off the property. God damn it. What a great addition to what was already stacking up to be the worst day he'd ever had. All he needed was the press snooping around.

He punched the sheriff's number in his cell phone.

"This is Brandt. I'm at Anne Mason's house. The media just got here. They must have caught wind of the second murder. Did you talk to Doc Meade about the autopsy results?"

"I was at the autopsy so I got the news firsthand," Miller said.

"Have you given any thought to what you'll say to the media?" asked Michael.

Miller scratched his head and said, "I'm scheduling a press conference for later this evening. The public needs to know this shit is happening in their community. We both know how that's going to go down."

"Afraid so." He imagined the panic that would ensue after people realized a serial killer was in their midst in this small farming community.

"I'm only giving them the bare minimum. They'll get nothing about the bleach, ribbon or anything like that." He shook his head and scratched his chin. Talking to the media was his least favorite job duty, and he was not looking forward to it. He was also not looking forward to the hit his department would take when the media found out they had no suspects. He prayed no one would find out the perp had slipped through the fingers of one of his deputies.

At the interstate rest stop, Anne stepped out of Hank's truck, pulled off the black baseball cap, and shook her now-blonde waves.

"Seems odd seeing you in blonde hair," said Hank.

"Thanks for picking up the hair color and other stuff on your way home. Most of all, thanks for helping me, Hank." She paused, scanning his face. "Are you sure you don't mind my using your personal truck?"

Hank usually drove one of her trucks with the Golden Acres Farm logo on the side. She knew his gleaming candy-red Ford F-150 truck was his baby, tucked away inside the garage most of the time. She could only remember seeing him drive it once, and that was to his interview.

"I trust you with it. Just stay safe, okay?"

"I will," she promised.

"We weren't followed, I've been checking since we left the farm. Clint will be here soon to take me back. What should I say to Mr. Brandt? I know he'll be looking for you."

"Tell him the truth. You don't know where I am." An important part of her plan was that no one, not even Hank, knew her destination.

"Okay. I'll take care of everything at the farm while you're gone." He just stood there with his hands in his pockets.

"I know you will, Hank." The worried look on his face made her feel guilty. She hugged him, jumped into the driver side of the truck, and adjusted the seat and rearview mirror. She pulled a folded map from her jacket pocket and laid it on the passenger seat. She'd plug the information into the GPS later.

He stood by her window. "Just keep checking your rearview mirror to see if anyone is following you, and if anyone does, drive to the nearest police station. Lock your doors."

She nodded, threw the truck into gear, and entered the

interstate, heading south. She had thirteen hours of driving ahead of her.

Hours later, Michael lay on the sofa in Anne's living room, staring at the ceiling. Once he'd installed the deadbolt lock on the back door, he'd decided to stay the night in case he got lucky and she returned. He also wouldn't mind a chance to catch the perp if he was crazy enough to try to get in the house again. Hank had still not returned and Michael wondered where in the hell he was. He had some questions for him—like where's Anne? He punched the pillow and tried to get comfortable. His cell phone vibrated in his pocket.

"Brandt."

"Michael, this is Frankie." "What did you find out?" Michael demanded, as he threw back a blanket and sat up.

"Afraid I have some bad news. There were no flight or car rental reservations in Anne's name. She didn't have time to get fake IDs, so I think we're safe in assuming she didn't fly or rent a car."

"Goddamn it!" he cursed. "I have to find her."

"I have an idea. I'm on the front porch. If you'll let me in, there is something I want to try."

Michael flung open the front door and ushered Frankie inside.

"Where's her computer?"

"In her study upstairs," he said. He bolted up the stairs with Frankie close behind.

Once in the study, Frankie turned on the computer then pulled up the Internet history, clicking on today's date. She scanned the list of web sites Anne had visited and clicked on MapQuest. When it populated the screen, she noticed that Anne was still signed in. She clicked on "saved maps".

"I know where she is going!" She flashed a grin at Michael, printed the map and said, "Savannah." He snatched the map out of her hand and raced down the stairs.

Chapter 10

"Hey, wait a minute!" Frankie sprinted after Michael and found him in the living room, throwing things into a duffle bag. "What are you doing?"

"What does it look like? I'm going after her." Michael pushed his wallet in his back pocket. Next he slid his gun in his waistband.

"Uh, boss, I thought that was my job." She watched him closely. She couldn't read his expression but she sensed he was caught off-guard by her statement.

"*I* need to go, Frankie."

He looked more worried than she had ever seen him. He was clearly personally involved with Anne Mason, and it was serious.

"Okay, let's sit down and talk about this." She needed to slow him down to think about the details involved to make this work.

"What's there to talk about?"

"First of all, there's your job. How are you going to explain rushing to Savannah to find a witness that you obviously have feelings for? Isn't this a conflict of interest or something?"

"You're right, and I intend to do something about that issue before I leave."

"About your mode of travel, I wouldn't fly or rent a car to go down there. It's too easy for someone to track and follow you."

"I'll drive."

"Okay, but keep a constant eye on the rearview mirror to make sure you're not being followed. The perp has been watching the house. He probably knows who you are. Undoubtedly, he knows what you drive. You could unknowingly lead him right to Anne."

"Shit." He rubbed his temples as the fragments of a headache fused in his brain.

Frankie pushed the hair out of her eyes, and then continued, "There are a few other things we need to discuss."

"Like what?" Patience was not his strong suit. The longer he stood here talking, the longer it would take him to get to Anne.

"Like the deputies watching the house. I take it you don't want them to know Anne is gone, do you? Once they find out, they'll be tracking their witness like bloodhounds."

"You're right."

"I've got something with me that I can attach to Anne's bedroom lamp so it goes on at a certain time, and shuts off at another. It will look like she's here in the house. It's a very temporary fix. It may not take long for them to figure it out." She rummaged in her purse until she found it. "Another issue is Deputy Hansen. He knows I watch the house from the field. I'll continue doing that until you return so he doesn't get suspicious. It will buy at least a little time until they realize she is gone."

"Thank you, Frankie. This means a lot to me."

"So what are you waiting for? Go."

Michael made a couple of calls from his cell phone as he raced to the interstate. His last call went to Helen, his career coach and State Attorney.

"Helen, this is Michael."

"Since it's late, this must be something important." There was something in his voice that made her uncomfortable.

"I made a decision that you're going to hear about. I'd like you to hear it from me." He didn't like disappointing Helen. She'd coached and supported him for a long time.

"Go on."

"I appointed a Special Prosecutor for the serial murder case we're working."

"Why in the hell did you do that? That case is probably the

biggest one you'll ever have. It's a career-maker. What were you thinking?"

"I appointed Edward Casey. He's on my staff. He has some relevant experiences and will do a good job."

"Who cares? That case was meant for *you.* Is it the girl? Is that what this is all about?" An uncomfortable silence ensued. He didn't respond, just like she knew he wouldn't.

"I'm taking a leave of absence. You can reach me by my cell if you need me."

"Michael, can't we talk about this?"

"No, Helen, there is nothing to talk about. It's my decision and I've made it."

In Savannah, Michael leaned against a red brick building on River Street, wearing a navy baseball cap, aviator sunglasses, and a black leather bomber jacket with jeans. He was doing some serious people watching and thought Anne would have been a hell of a lot easier to spot if she hadn't chosen a tourist-rich place like Savannah. He'd already seen a dozen women her height and weight maneuvering the cobblestone on River Street, going in and out of shops and restaurants—but no Anne.

He was ready to change directions and head toward the historic squares and parks when he spotted a tall woman with blonde, shoulder-length hair wearing dark sunglasses, a blue denim jacket and faded khakis duck inside a pet novelty shop. There was something familiar about her. He followed her inside and picked up a book about Labrador Retrievers. He peered over the top of the book to watch the woman who was now talking with a sales clerk. He moved a row closer and overheard the clerk ask her what kind of dog she had.

"I have a wonderful Giant Schnauzer named Harley. I'm looking for a sweater for him."

Bingo. The only woman he knew who would have that much affection in her voice for this type of dog was the one he wanted to pull into his arms right now. Relief shot through him. Anne was safe.

He was relieved, but he was still pissed. He couldn't believe she ran. She didn't trust him to protect her. Christ, the killer had been inside her house. Why wouldn't she trust him to keep her safe? Damn it, he thought they'd gotten closer than that. She takes off without a freaking word. Why would she do such a thing?

Michael left the store to lean against a tree near the entrance. He decided not to confront her until they were at a place that made it harder for her to escape him.

He followed her on River Street once she left the shop. He felt a coil of irritation twist inside his gut as he followed her a half-dozen blocks and not once had she looked around. He wasn't even trying to hide and she had no clue he was following her.

She entered a cobblestone alley, climbed a steep hill then walked through a small park before she crossed Bay Street and headed toward the historic squares. He followed her until she stopped in Forsyth Park near its large white fountain. He watched her sit on a bench in the shade of an oak tree drizzled with silver-spun Spanish moss. She fed pigeons with bits of sandwich bread she pulled out of her bag. She talked with a silver-haired lady with a small dog who stopped nearby. She smiled as she bent down to pet the dog, and Michael realized he couldn't remember the last time he saw her relaxed and smiling.

Anne watched the nice lady with the dog walk away. She loved being in Savannah. The place reminded her of her grandmother and the time they'd spent there. There wasn't a day that went by that she didn't think of her Grandma and how she'd stepped in when her nomad parents disappeared on yet another adventure. Adventures, it seemed, that were not possible with a small child afoot. So Anne was left behind, and her grandmother spent her golden years being mother to a grandchild whose parents left her in pursuit of excitement.

She'd only been in Savannah a day, but she already felt lonely. She missed Daisy, Hank and the farm. But most of all she missed Michael. She thought about the last night they spent together and began to crave him. There was no one like him, and the thought she was in love with him terrified her. She was obviously not a champion with relationships, or her marriage would have worked. She didn't think she could take another failure. She wondered if she could trust a man again. She'd trusted Allan completely, which enabled him to lie to her time and again. Could she trust Michael?

Her stomach began to growl. When was the last time she'd eaten? She picked up her shopping bags and walked back toward her hotel on Bay Street.

Anne entered the dark hotel room and threw her shopping bags and purse on the bed. She heard the low groan of a tanker ship coming down the Savannah River, and walked to the French doors to open the drapes. Afternoon sunlight filled the room as she watched the giant beast glide effortlessly through the water. Stacks and stacks of railroad cars lined the first level, and workers moved about.

She needed to freshen up before she went out seeking food, so she turned to go to the bathroom. There was movement in the shadows in the corner of the room that caught her eye. She froze and reached for the gun at the back of her waist that was not there. Damn. She'd left it in the truck.

"Nice room, Anne. I especially like the French balconies facing the river. The hardwood floors and four-poster bed is nothing to sneeze at either." He kept his voice low and controlled, trying to hide the anger that swelled within.

"Michael?" This was impossible. How could he know she was here? How could he be here?

"I'm glad you still remember my name." A thin chill hung on his words.

"How did you get in my room?"

"It's surprising how quickly hotel clerks believe the husband-planning-an-anniversary-surprise-for-his-wife-in-town-for-business story. I guess it made it all that more believable that I was holding roses. I brought them up earlier." He pointed to a large bouquet of yellow roses on a chest near the bathroom.

"How did you know I was here?"

"It helped that you used your real name." He shot her an icy glare that made her legs quiver. She had never seen him so angry.

"No, I mean, how did you know I was in Savannah? I didn't tell anyone."

"You forget I used to be a cop."

She just looked at him.

"Actually, the big question for me is which part of recent events pissed me off the most." He shifted in the chair and she nearly jumped back. He pushed forward and leaned on his elbows. "Was it making love for the first time, after which you announce your plan not to see me until after the perp's trial? Keep in mind, we have no idea who the perp is, let alone arrest him and try him."

"Michael, I had good reasons…"

"No, you didn't," he interrupted. "Let me go on. So you hire Lane Hansen to protect you instead of me. Next, I find out the killer is in your field watching your house, waiting until he can get to you. Then I find out another body has been found on your property, and for one agonizing hour, I think it might be you. But do you let me stay with you and protect you that night? No, of course not, it's not in your freaking plan. So what happens later that night, the perp is found not only *in* your house, but outside your bedroom door. And where am I? Oh yeah, I'm at home as you demanded."

"May I talk now?"

"No. So then I find you've implemented a *new* plan and disappeared. So I spend the next thirteen hours driving here. You scared the crap out of me. I didn't know if he followed you, if I would find you here alive or not." He rose, pulled off his leather jacket and threw it on the bed. He pulled his revolver out of his waistband and placed it on the end table near his chair then sat back down.

"Michael, I'm so sorry." She inched toward him. He looked so worried and weary it tugged at her heart. She reached his chair and looked down at him. He pushed back to look up at her, so she took the opportunity to lower herself to sit in his lap. His large arms flew around her and held her so tight she could barely breathe.

Suddenly Lady Gaga's "Telephone" tune rang out, and Anne pulled her cell out of her purse to check a text. She moved near the window.

"That's odd. I've got a text from Richard Thompson. I haven't heard from him in months—not since I sold him my shares in the company."

"What's going on?"

"He says he needs to see me right away in person. He has something to tell me."

"What?"

"I don't know. This is not like Richard. We text and email all the time but he says he wants to talk to me in person before he goes to the police."

"Call him, Anne."

She let the phone ring until finally she reached Richard's voice mail. "Richard, I got your text. Please call me as soon as you get this message."

Something was wrong. What did he have to tell her that he could only do in person? Why was he involving the police? It made no sense.

Michael's cell buzzed in his pocket. He pulled it out of his pocket and checked the display. It was Edward Casey, his deputy prosecutor.

"Michael, I've got an update for you.

"I hope you're about to tell me they've found some evidence tying the killer to Cindy Barrett."

"No. The sheriff knows Anne is not at the house. He says he will arrest you both if you don't return within 48 hours. He's serious, Michael. I know she's with you and you have to bring her back."

"Easier said than done."

"The FBI is involved now. An agent called me this morning. He wants to interview Anne. You've got to get her back to Indiana. I'll schedule a meeting in your office. Just let me know when you will be here."

Michael disconnected the call and watched Anne as her laptop came to life.

"What are you doing?"

"I need to see a photo of Cindy Barrett. I don't know why, but her name sounds familiar." She typed in the news web address and saw the headline: Another Body Found on Farm. She scrolled down until she could see the photo. "I *have* seen her before. But I don't know where or under what circumstances." She closed the laptop. Are the killings random or are they connected somehow? She needed to find out and soon.

"Michael, what do you know about Cindy Barrett?"

"She was a thirty-year-old high school teacher in Fountain County. She'd been missing for about a month. She died the same way as Rachel Mitchell—strangulation. The crime scene techs are hoping they'll find fingerprints on the ribbon wrapped around her, but that's doubtful. He probably used gloves like last time."

"There has to be a connection between the two victims and me. I have to find out what that is."

"Anne, we need to talk," said Michael. Forcing her to return to Indiana wasn't a high point on his list of conversations, but it had to happen.

"Are you hungry?" she asked.

"Honey, for you I'm always hungry." He gave her a lusty grin and she popped him on the arm. "But we need to talk."

"I mean for food. I'm starving. Can't we get something to eat before 'the talk'? When was the last time you ate?"

"I can't remember." The thirteen hour drive, lack of sleep and food was starting to hit him. He could definitely use some food.

"Let's walk to the City Market. There are some great restaurants there."

He watched her brush her hair in the mirror then reach into her purse for some lip gloss. God, she was beautiful. Every time he looked at her his senses went on alert.

"Am I going to get my redhead back?" He moved behind her, placing his hands on her waist.

"I thought blondes were supposed to have more fun and that *all* men were crazy for blondes."

"Not this one."

He pulled his leather jacket on and reached for his gun.

"Is the gun really necessary here, Michael?"

"Hell yes. I don't think I was followed, but I've learned with this sick bastard that anything is possible." He scowled at her and asked, "What about you? Were you followed?"

"No, I wasn't."

"How can you be so sure?"

"I kept an eye on the rearview mirror all the way down here."

"You were followed, Anne."

"What?" She gasped and stared at him.

"You were followed on River Street all afternoon and you had no clue. You didn't even check to make sure you weren't being followed."

"You followed me?" She bit her lip as she remembered shopping on River Street. She had experienced a sense of freedom she hadn't felt in a long time. It had felt so good, nothing else mattered. But safety should have. Forgetting safety measures is what got her carjacked. He looked pissed again, so she pulled him by his jacket and kissed him to distract him. She felt him tense so she melted against him, threw her arms around his neck and pulled him down into another kiss. This time he hauled her against him and kissed her hard until she felt the heat of it all the way to her toes. He broke off the kiss and gently pushed her back.

"Are you hungry or not? I'm asking because in about a minute, you're going to be flat on your back on that bed with a very aroused man on top of you."

She grinned and moved toward the door. He pulled her back and checked the hallway before he led her out.

Once at the City Market, they held hands and reviewed the menu of each restaurant. It was unseasonably warm and the spicy scent of hot cheese pizza wafted around Vinnie Van Go-Go's. They noticed several couples sitting outside the restaurant, devouring gooey slices of pizza and drinking cold beer. A rock band was setting up its speakers and instruments down the street past the horse carriage rides. Anne and Michael decided no matter where they ate, they wanted to be outside to enjoy the incredible weather.

Belford's of Savannah restaurant was located across the street, and once they read the menu, the decision was made. The spicy aroma of sea food and steak besieged them, and both were ravenous. The waitress found them a table under the awning outside, then brought them tall glasses of sweet ice tea with their menus.

"I'm glad we chose Belford's," said Anne. "I've been here

before, but it has been a long time. This building was originally the home to a wholesale food company."

"Really? How did you know that?"

"My grandma was from Savannah and used to have a house here."

"I didn't know that. There is a lot about you that I don't know, but I want to."

"I love Savannah. I wish I had been able to keep Grandma's house, but I was in college when she died. I didn't have the money to keep it."

He looked at her thoughtfully, but didn't say anything. He had the urge to contact local realtors to find out if the house was available.

"What?"

"Nothing." He looked down at his menu. "So what's good here?"

"Everything."

The waitress returned and Michael ordered fried green tomatoes and crab cakes for appetizers.

"Fried green tomatoes, huh? I think you know me better than you think." That he remembered how much she liked fried green tomatoes touched her heart. He could be so thoughtful. She squeezed his hand.

"Great table for people watching, isn't it?" He tried to keep it light as he scanned the crowd, looking for anyone that was paying too much attention to them.

"Who's Edward Casey? I saw his name on your cell phone display when he called."

"He is one of my deputy prosecutors. I assigned him to the murders before I left Indiana."

"You did what? Why did you do that?" After all she'd done to protect his career, how could he make a decision like that?

"It was *my* decision, Anne. He's a damn good prosecutor. He's had cases like this in the past, and he's always won. I'm his supervisor, so I'll still be very involved."

"You made this decision because of me because *I'm* your conflict of interest." Her eyes glistened with tears. She felt sick with guilt.

"There were so many aspects of this case that were getting too complicated, and the job was getting in the way of what *I* wanted and needed to do. It was a good decision and it was mine to make. Stop blaming yourself."

"I don't want to hurt your career."

"You're not." He paused as he scanned her face. He might as well tell her everything. "I'm taking a leave of absence. I don't even know if I want this job or this career. I've been obsessed with my job for years, with little time for a personal life. I need some time and balance."

"I get it. I felt the same way when I sold the shares of my computer company." She looked at him thoughtfully. They weren't so different after all. "Are you going to tell me why Edward Casey called?"

"The sheriff knows you left. He's going to arrest us both if we don't return within 48 hours."

"Seriously?" She was reminded of just how much she disliked Sheriff Miller.

"Edward says he's very serious. The FBI is involved now. He wants to interview you. Edward is setting up a meeting."

"When should do we leave?"

"Sometime tomorrow. Shall we use Hank's truck or mine?"

"How did you know I have Hank's truck?"

"You were last seen with Hank so I put it together. How about if we leave Hank's truck here and I fly someone down to drive it back?"

"Okay. Can we *not* talk about this anymore tonight?"

They had precious little time left in Savannah, and she wanted to enjoy every second. Who knew what waited for them when they returned to Indiana? If the killer had his way, these moments would be the last she had with Michael or anyone else.

"You've got a deal," said Michael. "Let's talk about you." She was right. They had more than enough time to talk about things during the drive back.

"What do you want to know?" she asked.

"What were you like in college?" He wanted to know

everything about her, but he was satisfied with starting here.

"I was a computer geek. I worked my way through college, and when I wasn't working, I was studying. I didn't have time for much of a social life. I met Allan in my senior year in one of my classes."

"And after college?"

"I worked for a couple of companies in their I.S. departments. A few years ago, Richard and I started Computer Solutions, Inc. It took a lot of time and hard work for the start-up, but it was worth it. By the time I left the company, we'd added a department of technicians for at-home computer repair. It was pretty popular."

He could tell by her expression how much her company had meant to her. And he'd helped Allan take it away from her. The guilt was palpable.

The appetizers arrived and the rock band started playing. Anne lifted a fried green tomato with her fork and placed it on Michael's plate. He placed a couple of crab cakes on her plate. He thought of how comfortable it was to be with her.

"Oh, my God, these fried green tomatoes are heaven." She closed her eyes, leaned back in her chair and moaned with pleasure. "So are the crab cakes."

The food was amazing and it didn't take them much time to finish off the appetizers, then the main course.

"How about a carriage ride?" Michael suggested. The meal was over but he didn't want this time with her to end. She seemed more at ease than she had been in a long, long time.

He watched as she leaned toward him, placing her hand on his thigh. Her eyes had a smoldering look and there was no mistake about what she was thinking. Lust filled his veins, surging down to his belly.

"Let's go back to the hotel," she whispered.

He kissed her hard and Anne pulled at his shirt in the elevator. She was desperate to touch him. When they got to the room, it was dark except for slivers of moonlight cutting through the window. He laid his revolver on a table and pulled her to the bed.

The next morning, he made arrangements for Ted to fly down to get Hank's truck. They were headed North on I-95 before noon. Michael drove as Anne searched her phone for a voice mail or another text from Richard. There was nothing. She couldn't stop thinking about him and why he sent her such an odd text. What did he have to tell her that he could only say in person?

Michael's cell phone buzzed and he pressed the speaker button. He wanted Anne to trust him, and sharing information was part of the plan.

"Michael, this is Ed Casey. I'm afraid I have news."

"From the sound of your voice, the news isn't good." He glanced at Anne. Maybe sharing this particular information wasn't the best idea.

"There's been another murder. The body was found this morning about 100 feet away from where Cindy Barrett was found in the Wind Farm construction area of Anne's farm."

"Was it another woman?"

"No, the body is male. His wallet was in his back pocket so we have identification. His name is Richard Thompson." Michael's eyes flew to Anne.

Anne cried, "No!" She covered her face with her hands and sobbed. Not Richard. Oh, my God. Why is this happening?

"I'll call you back." Michael pulled off the road and pulled Anne into his arms.

"Richard was such a good guy. He would do anything for anyone. His employees loved him. Who could have done this?"

"I don't know, honey. But I think we're close to finding out. We now know there is a connection. That sick fuck dumped Richard's body on your land, just like he did the other victims. There has to be a tie from the victims to your company and to you. That's the only thing that makes sense now."

"Michael, please get off at the next exit that has a Starbucks. I have to do some research on my laptop, and need their Wi-Fi connection."

"Sure." He shoved the gear in drive and headed down the interstate, scanning each sign they encountered.

"I have to get into the company's database. I want to find out what Richard didn't get the chance to tell me."

They found a Starbucks, and Anne opened her laptop at a table near a window while Michael ordered coffee. Once she got to the Internet, she typed in the company website. On the home page, she signed in as an employee. She held her breath and prayed they hadn't removed her access because she was no longer employed there. A second later, the customer database sprang to life.

Michael sat down, stared at the screen, and slid a mocha latte to Anne. "I see you got into the database. What are you looking for?"

"I'm going to plug in each victim's name to see if they were former clients." She typed Rachel Mitchell's name in the search box and tapped ENTER. In a second, Rachel's account appeared. "Michael, look. Rachel Mitchell had an account. It says here that she had a problem with her hard drive last April. Technician #26 went to her house. It looks like the repair was made and she paid the invoice."

"Now look for Cindy Barrett."

She typed Cindy's name in the search box and pressed ENTER. Her account appeared. "She has an account too. She had a service call last March. Technician #26 was sent. The repair was made and she paid the invoice."

"So the same technician was sent to both victims' homes?"

"Yes." She gasped. Oh, God, is this a connection to the victims? To her? Is this what Richard was trying to tell her?

Michael pulled out his cell phone. He was ready to press the button to the sheriff's office. "Who is Technician #26? What's his name?"

"I don't know."

"What do you mean you don't know? How many employees did you have?"

"When I left, we had three hundred employees. I didn't know all of them. I was lucky to know all the people in my own department. I was spending a lot of time on software design." She paused, still stunned. Her heart was racing. She had to calm down so she could think clearly. "Richard ran the computer repair department. I have no idea how many technicians he had."

"Do you have a way to find out who Technician #26 is?"

"No. I don't have access to the confidential employee files. Only Human Resources has access." She took a deep breath. Images and thoughts were bouncing around in her head making no connections. "Michael, is it possible that an employee in my company murdered two of our clients? If so, what's the motive? And what's my connection? Why were the bodies dumped on *my* land?"

Michael pushed his chair closer to her and put his arm around her. He scanned her face; she had paled and had a panicky look in her eyes. "I don't know, honey. But I think we're getting very close."

She pulled out her cell phone. Marta Williams was in charge of Human Resources. She would have the information she needed about the technician.

"Marta, this is Anne." Michael leaned closer so he could hear the conversation.

"Oh, God, Anne, have you heard about Richard? We've had to send people home. They were too upset to work. I can't stop crying. Why Richard? I still can't believe it."

"Marta, I am so sorry. But I need to ask you some questions. Did Richard ask you for information about one of his technicians recently?"

"Yes, funny you should ask. Last week, he came in my office, closed the door and asked for an employee file."

"Whose file did you give him?"

"I can't remember. I was so surprised that Richard asked for an employee file, that I just dug it out and handed it to him."

"Marta, it's important you find that file. I need the employee's name. It's urgent. Please go to Richard's office to see if you can find it. Call me back."

"Of course, Anne. I'll look right now."

Anne closed her laptop, grabbed her purse and headed toward the truck with Michael close behind. "We have to get back to Indiana as quickly as we can, before anyone else is hurt."

They'd crossed North Carolina's state line when Anne's cell phone sounded. She pressed the speaker button.

"This is Marta. I'm sorry it took so long. First, I couldn't find the key to Richard's office. Once I got in, his office was a mess so I had to sift through a lot of papers before I recognized the employee file."

"So you found it?"

"Yes. I remember this guy. I wish Richard had talked to me. This is a technician that Richard had to fire. We'd gotten complaints from a couple of female clients. They said the technician made inappropriate remarks to them during the repair visit. If that wasn't enough, he started sending them sexually explicit emails and texts. They both said they saw him sitting in his truck outside their houses at night, weeks after the repair visit. They were really afraid of him."

"They were wise to fear him."

"We had a meeting with him discussing the allegations before we terminated him. It was ugly. He got really emotional. He was screaming and crying. He said the women were lying. We fired him that day. We felt we had no choice. We can't have an employee go into customers' homes with those kind of complaints lodged against him."

"I don't remember this at all."

"No, I don't doubt it. Richard told me that you were too busy to attend the meeting and not to bother you with it. I came to your office to get your signature on the termination paperwork per company policy. You were so swamped that day; I don't think you even realized what you were signing."

"Who is the employee, Marta?"

"Charles Beatty. He was with the company for about a year."

"Is there a photo of him in the file?"

"No, I already looked. But I think I know where I can get one."

"When you find it, I want you to fax it to Michael Brandt's office. Hold on while I give you the number. We'll pick it up when we get to Indiana." She paused and looked at Michael. "Marta, we're going to call the sheriff's office and get you some protection. Lock up and don't leave the office until you hear from me. You may be as much the killer's target as I am."

"Anne, are you thinking Charles Beatty murdered Richard?" asked Marta. Icy fear twisted inside her.

"Yes. I also think he killed Rachel Mitchell and Cindy Barrett and left their bodies on my farm."

"Oh, I've got to sit down." "Make sure everything is locked up and stay there until you hear from me." Anne disconnected the call.

Michael dialed Edward Casey.

"I need your help. I think I know who the murderer is. Please conference Sheriff Miller in. He needs to hear this." Ten minutes later, he disconnected the call.

"You heard that. Sheriff Miller's putting an APB out on Beatty. He's getting a deputy over to Marta as soon as he can."

Michael hoped to hell that Charles Beatty was in police custody by the time they returned, so this nightmare would be over.

Chapter 11

They were an hour away from Indianapolis, when Michael pulled a photo from the inside of his jacket and handed it to Anne.

"What's this?"

"It's a picture of my lake house near Rockville."

"It's beautiful. I love all the windows, the tall trees, and the lake view."

"No one knows I own it. I bought it about three months before I took the prosecutor job. Let me take you there so you'll be safe. We can go after your interview with the FBI agent today."

"Why can't I go home?"

"It's not safe. Beatty has no problem breaking into your house, or going to your farm to dump bodies, security or not. No one knows about this lake house. It will be your safe house until all this is over. That's where you are going to stay, Anne. I'm not taking no for an answer."

"Okay, I'll stay at the lake house," she said and made a vow to make it a lot harder for Charles Beatty to get to her.

He sighed with relief. He was sure she would fight harder to go home.

"I've been thinking about something, Anne. Why didn't Charles Beatty bother to hide the bodies or bury them?"

"I don't know."

"I do. I think his rage is more important to him than getting caught. That makes him very dangerous. His sense of anger is overriding his need for personal safety and freedom. His need to communicate his anger to *you* is overwhelming."

"If you are trying to scare me, you're succeeding."

"Good. I want you to pay more attention to your safety than you did in Savannah, Anne. Remember that self-defense class you told me you took?"

"Yes."

"Think about some of the techniques you were taught. Think about what you can do to protect yourself if this guy gets to you and I'm not around."

He was right. She had avoided injury from her carjacker by remembering the self-defense techniques she learned in her class.

"Get your gun out of the glove box. Put it in your purse along with your pepper spray."

She looked at Michael as she pushed the Glock into her purse. There was an inherent strength in his face. She had never met anyone so strong and determined. Being with him had become the only place she felt safe.

"Hey, are you checking me out again?" He grinned and moved his arm across her seat. He needed to see her smile again.

She rolled her eyes and looked out the window.

She wondered what he thought about her. How did he feel about her? There had been one drama after the other since they met. Most men hated drama in relationships. He was probably sick of it, and she didn't blame him.

She was in love with him. When she found him in her hotel room in Savannah, she knew how much. He'd driven all that way to find and protect her. No one had done anything even close to that for her—ever. She knew that he cared for her and was attracted to her; but she needed to know he was in love with her. A man could care about a woman and want to protect her, but that didn't mean he was in love with her. Some men were hard-wired to protect a woman, even if he wasn't emotionally involved with her. Was Michael one of those men?

She watched him tap a button on his cell phone.

"Edward, does the agent still want to talk to Anne? Okay, we'll be there in about an hour." He disconnected the call then called Sheriff Miller.

"This is Michael Brandt. Have you apprehended Charles Beatty?"

"I sent the SWAT team to his house this morning. It was empty. Found a neighbor who doesn't think he's lived there for weeks. I've got every deputy on my team looking for the bastard. We'll get him. Where the hell are you anyway?"

"Coming back. Be there in an hour. Keep me updated."

His next call was to Frankie.

"Hi, boss. I heard we have a name for our perp."

"His name is Charles Beatty. I need you to find him."

"Hansen told me early this morning that the SWAT team was going to hit his house."

"They did, but no Beatty. House was empty. Find out where else he could be living."

"I'm on it, Boss."

Michael disconnected the call and focused on the road.

"Who's Frankie?"

"Frankie Douglas is a private investigator. She's done a lot of work for me in the past when I was a defense attorney."

"What is Frankie doing for you now?"

Judging by her tone, Michael knew he could be in some trouble here.

"I hired her to protect you when you wouldn't let *me*. She has been watching your house every night." He glanced at Anne to study her reaction.

"What does she look like?"

"She's a tall woman with blonde hair."

"I think I've met Frankie, but she introduced herself to me as a deputy with the sheriff department. Why would she do that?"

"She's good with confidentiality. I told her to keep this job under wraps."

"Why didn't you tell me you hired her to protect me?" She wanted to be a lot more annoyed than she was. How can you be mad at a man whose goal is to protect your life? "It would be refreshing if you'd involve me on decisions like this."

"You'd already pushed me out. Why would I think you would agree with me about hiring Frankie? You'd already hired Lane Hansen."

She shrugged and looked out the window.

"Have you and Frankie had a thing?" She'd seen the tall, curvy blonde and she was beautiful. Jealousy shot through her like a gun. The visual of him with another woman was unbearable.

"Not a chance. Anything between Frankie and me is strictly business. She's damn good at what she does. That's why I trusted her to protect you." He grasped her hand, intertwining his fingers with hers.

Edward Casey welcomed them when they arrived at Michael's office. They sat around a small conference table as Edward's secretary delivered hot cups of coffee. He gazed at Anne, immediately recognizing her as the woman Michael asked him about at the bar. No wonder Michael was so taken with her. She was beautiful.

"I'm glad you arrived early. I want to give you both an update," Edward began. "We were able to get a partial fingerprint from the neck of his last victim, Richard Thompson. The sheriff ran it through IAFIS, the national fingerprint and criminal history system. Unfortunately, Charles Beatty is not in the system. However, we now have a partial to match with his fingerprint once he is captured."

Edward Casey noticed a man in a navy suit and white shirt standing in the doorway. He stood and offered his hand to shake.

"You must be Agent Smith."

Agent Smith shook his hand and gave a small nod of acknowledgement to the group then sat at the only empty chair at the conference table. He looked hard at Anne.

"The Bureau is now involved in the case, and I've been given the assignment. We believe we have a serial killer at work. It's my job to catch him."

"Are you saying the Sheriff's department is no longer involved in the case?" Michael asked.

"That's correct. The Bureau has more resources and manpower to deal with serial killers than the local police. We'll take it from here."

"Anne, I understand that you have a theory about Charles Beatty."

"Yes, I do. He's an ex-employee, a computer technician who was furious about being fired from my company. He worked on computers in the homes of two of the victims. Both women filed complaints about him. His last victim, Richard Thompson, was his supervisor at the time of his firing." Anne swallowed hard and tried to force back the tears that formed at the thought that Richard and the others were dead.

"I'll consider your theory as well as others. I'm having a profile created by our Behavioral Analysis Unit. I should receive that by tomorrow."

"I'd like my office to have a copy of the profile. Please get it to Edward." Michael said. "He's the assigned prosecutor on this case. We'll also need the name of your profiler. We may use him or her as a potential expert witness at the trial." Michael looked at Edward Casey, who nodded. "What information do *you* have about Beatty?"

"Mr. Beatty does not have a criminal record, nor did he serve in the armed forces. He is thirty-six years old and divorced. He attended college, but dropped out after six months. He worked at one other computer company before joining Ms. Mason's. His parents are dead. I'm not one hundred percent sure he is our perp."

"But you're still looking at him, right?" Anne looked at the agent as if he had two heads. How could he not be sure Beatty was the killer? All signs pointed directly to him.

"Yes, I am." He gave his answer to the group. Then he focused his attention back on Anne. "Ms. Mason, if you are ready. I'd like to get our interview started."

He slid a white sheet of paper across the table to Edward and Michael. "You'll find my cell phone number and other contact information on this paper. You will also find the address of the office we've rented for this project. This is where our interview will take place."

"Wait a minute. Why can't your interview with Anne take place here in my offices?" Michael demanded. Narrowing his eyes, he glared at the agent. There was no way he wanted Anne out of his sight.

"It's a Bureau policy. In addition, there are two other agents who will participate in the interview. They're waiting for us back at the office."

He Smith stood and motioned for Anne to join him. "I'll drive Ms. Mason back in a couple of hours. We should be finished by no later than six o'clock."

Michael watched them walk down the hall to the elevator. He turned to Edward Casey, "I don't like this a bit. If he doesn't have her back by six o'clock, I'm going to kick his FBI ass."

Edward chuckled as he left the room. Michael turned his computer on to read his emails and get some work done while he waited. Hours passed and he heard nothing from FBI Agent Smith.

Near the door, Michael's fax machine hummed to announce the arrival of a new fax. He ignored the sound until he heard the rustle of paper landing on the hardwood floor. He bent down to retrieve the three-sheet fax. He picked up one page that made his heart stop. He was looking at a photo of Charles Beatty, whose image was identical to that of FBI Agent Charles Smith.

He raced to Edward Casey's office. "Did you check out this FBI agent?"

"No. Why would I? He's FBI."

"He's *not* FBI!" Michael slammed the photo on Edward's desk. "We just handed over Anne to the killer! Shit. We have no idea where he took her. Even though the office address he gave us may be phony, call the sheriff and get some deputies over to that office address ASAP."

He rushed back to his office and retrieved his cell phone to call Frankie.

"Frankie, Beatty has Anne. He pretended to be an FBI Agent and took her from my office. How can I find her?"

"Hold on while I get online and get into one of my programs. There is a good chance I can track her by the GPS in her cell phone. Where are you?"

"I'm in my office."

"Stay there. I'm coming over. Don't take off by yourself."

Agent Smith led Anne to what he told her was the typical car issued by the Bureau, a white late model Ford Taurus. She pulled the seatbelt across her waist, and waited for him to start the engine.

Smith drove down Main Street then turned on Grant Street where there was a long line of shopping plazas and small businesses. He didn't talk, which was fine with Anne. She just wanted to get to his office and get this interview over with. Better yet, she wanted Charles Beatty apprehended and this damn nightmare to be over.

Before long, he pulled into what looked like an abandoned shopping plaza. Anne shifted in her seat and asked, "This is where you rented an office?"

"Yes. The Bureau has me on a tight budget and I got good rates on rent here."

He drove to the back of the building and stopped near a loading ramp. He got out of the car and moved around to the passenger door to open it for Anne.

"Come this way," he said. When they reached the back of the car, he motioned for her to wait. "I need to get my briefcase out of the trunk."

Anne scanned the empty parking lot and wondered why the FBI would choose such an isolated place for a temporary office. Sudden, sharp pain fired from her neck then shot throughout her body. She cried out as her legs collapsed and she dropped to the pavement. Her entire body started jerking with agony as spasms racked her muscles. What had he done to her, and why?

"It's time to get you into the trunk, bitch." He scooped Anne up and dropped her into the trunk, and moved her legs and arms until she was lying in a fetal position. Her vision blurred as paralysis overtook her muscles. She heard the slamming of the trunk lid and darkness claimed her.

Exhaustion pulled at Anne as she struggled for consciousness. She was still unable to fully process what had happened and where she was. Sometime later, she remembered being in Agent Smith's car. They stopped. Where was she?

Frankie raced into his office, dropped her duffle bag on the floor and handed Michael her cell phone. "I've got her. I was right; we can track her by the GPS in her cell phone. Look at the display. Right now she's on Grant Street." He sprinted down the stairs with Frankie close behind until they reached his truck.

"What if he's already killed her?" Michael's fingers tightened around the steering wheel as slivers of fear cut through him. He didn't know what he would do if Beatty hurt her. Who was he kidding? Beatty was a sick, angry bastard who had already killed three people he thought wronged him. Anne was his next target. Beatty wouldn't hurt her. He would *kill* her. There was no doubt. If she died, he vowed to personally track Beatty and there would be no need for a fucking trial. The bastard would be eliminated and the world would be a better place.

"It's not the way he works. Remember, Michael, he kept Rachel Mitchell for over a month before he killed her. We've got to keep believing we have time." She scanned his face and wished she'd jumped into the driver seat first. He looked like he was going to explode.

Her cell phone vibrated and she fished it out of her purse. She prayed it was Ted telling her that her hunch about Beatty renting a car for his disguise as an agent was on target. She saw his name flash on the phone display.

"Ted, did you find out anything from the car rental agencies?"

"We struck pay dirt. The prick rented a 2006 white Ford Taurus. License plate is Indiana 475 BBB. Did you get that?"

"Yes. Now do me a favor and call Sheriff Miller and give him this information. We're tracking her by GPS now." She looked at her cell phone display. "She's leaving Council Street heading toward State Route 41."

"No problem. Be safe, Frankie."

Michael touched her arm and said, "Don't disconnect. Get Ted to check the property records online in public records. See if Beatty had any recent real estate transactions. The SWAT team found his house empty, but he has to be living somewhere."

Anne tried to shift to a more comfortable position. The thick cloud of confusion abandoned her brain, leaving comprehension in its wake. It was very dark, but she realized she was in the trunk of

Agent Smith's car. Thank God, he hadn't tied her up. She could hear the road beneath her, bumps in the pavement jarring her body. Why in the hell would an FBI Agent put her in the trunk of his car? It made no sense.

She regained feeling in her arms and legs. She stretched her fingers as well as her arms and legs as much as she could in the small space. She must get to her purse. Her cell phone was there as was her container of pepper spray and her Glock. The strap still crossed her body but the purse itself was somewhere behind her. She moved her hands behind herself as far as they would stretch, but found no purse. Where had it gone?

She tried rolling to her right side, but the small trunk permitted little movement. She pushed as far as she could, and then extended her arms behind her body again searching for the purse. At last, she felt the strap. Inch by inch, she pulled the purse closer. Soon she could feel the sewn edge of the purse. Suddenly the car stopped, slamming her face against the hard metal frame of the trunk.

"Frankie, Sheriff Miller gave me your message and I'm in pursuit." Deputy Lane Hansen growled. "Where are you?"

Frankie held her cell phone to her ear. "We're on State Road 41 going south. We're in Michael Brandt's truck and we just passed Route 234."

"Okay, I'm about seven miles behind you. I'm turning on the siren now to pass these cars so I can gain more speed. Hope to catch up with you soon. Any idea where he's headed?"

"Not a clue."

Charles Beatty opened the car trunk and peered inside. "Why Anne, how did you get a bloody nose? Too freaking bad. I stopped to check on you to make sure you were all right. I wouldn't want anything to happen to you before we get to the house. I have that private party planned for the two of us. I've waited a long time for this. Now keep on being a good girl so I don't have to use the stun gun on you again."

He slammed the trunk lid, and before long the car was moving, and Anne heard the road sounds again.

Private party? Waiting a long time? My God, he's not a FBI agent. He's Charles Beatty! Panic like she'd never known before welled in her throat. She began to shake as terrifying images of his plans for her formed in her mind. He would kill her like he did the others.

Anger soon replaced the fear. This sick bastard killed one of her best friends and two innocent women. She had no time to be afraid; she needed to plan how she'd stop him. The first item on her plan was to get her cell phone out of her purse to call for help. She moved her hands behind her as far as they would stretch and felt the edge of her purse. Carefully, she tried to secure the purse by embedding her long fingernails in the sewn edge and pressing down against the flooring. It moved slightly. She clawed at it until it moved closer. She felt an opening and moved her fingers inside. A painful cramp claimed her arm.

He would kill her. She knew it. She was going to die. Her mind was a swirl of memories. Her first day at school—her grandmother teaching her to ride a bicycle—graduating from college—spending time with Marion—the first time Michael made love to her.

Michael. There were so many things about Michael she loved, like his fierce need to protect her, the way he smiled when he told her about his favorite things, and his mischievous expression when he teased her. She imagined his eyes filled with desire when they made love.

Why had she not told him that she was in love with him? She had every opportunity to tell him in Savannah, but she hadn't. Now she may never get the chance.

Michael pressed the speaker button on his cell phone. Ted's voice filled the car.

"Michael, your idea to check public records was a good one. Beatty's maternal grandmother died two months ago and he inherited her old farm house outside of Bainbridge. He's trying to sell it so I'm looking at the house now on the realtor's site on the

Internet. The house is located just before you reach Bainbridge on State Road 36. There is a white mailbox with the name 'Griffin' painted in large black letters. There's also a realtor sign in the front yard."

"That has to be where he's headed. Anything else?" Michael's pulse kicked up a notch. He now had a chance of finding the bastard before he hurt Anne.

"Yeah, the house is about a quarter mile off the road. The left side section of the property is wooded. You should be able to approach the house by foot without him seeing you."

Michael disconnected the call and glanced at Frankie.

"State Road 36 is about fifteen minutes away." She reached for her duffle bag in the back seat. She unzipped it and pulled out her Glock 21 and slipped an extra magazine in her pocket. She tucked the pistol in her shoulder holster, then looked at Michael. "Do you have your gun with you?"

In response, he opened his jacket, revealing the revolver tucked into the waistband of his jeans. "We'll drive by his house first and get a sense of the layout of the property. Then we'll hide the truck and approach on foot."

"Looking forward to it." Frankie looked straight ahead, her brows drawn together in an angry frown. She pulled out her cell to call Deputy Hansen.

"Hansen, we've got a location."

"No shit. How'd you pull that off?"

"I just used some superior investigative skills." She couldn't resist needling him. She knew he was on the SWAT Team who discovered Beatty's house was empty. She'd heard that Lane and every other deputy in the department were looking for Beatty, but with no success.

"Sure you did. Where is he headed?"

"He's taking State Road 36 toward Bainbridge. Look for a farm house just before you get to town on the right side of the road. There is a white mailbox near the road with the name 'Griffin' painted in large black letters. There's also a realtor sign in the front yard."

"Okay. Got it."

"One more thing, Hansen."

"What's that?"

"Turn off your freaking siren. He may panic and kill her if he hears you coming. We're driving past the house then hiding the truck in the woods. We're approaching the house on foot."

"You're not doing a damn thing until I get there. Do you understand?" Lane disconnected the call and chuckled. If there was one thing that made him hot for a woman, it was a sassy attitude. And this woman had more attitude and sass than anyone he'd ever met.

Anne felt the car turn onto what felt like a gravel road. Her body bumped around in the trunk until her teeth rattled. It wasn't long until the car and the sound of the motor stopped.

Clutching the container of pepper spray in hand, her body stiffened as she waited for the trunk lid to open. She heard footsteps, then heard the latch of the trunk lid as it twisted. He pushed the lid up and looked at Anne. She lay very still, until he pulled at her arm. She pointed the pepper spray container at his face and pressed down on the button as hard as she could. He screamed as the toxic spray gushed into his face. He knocked the container out of her hand. Pain exploded in her left jaw as Beatty backhanded her. Blood sprayed from her nose and lips. She waited for another blow but he dropped to the ground rubbing his eyes and cursing.

She pulled herself to a sitting position, surprised at how weak she felt. She got herself out of the trunk and tried to stand but her rubbery legs refused to hold her up and she dropped to the ground near Beatty. He grabbed her arm and she kicked him in the mid-section. Her gun. Where was her gun? She rummaged through the purse to find it.

She saw his stun gun just before the probes hit her neck. For a second, it felt like a horse kicked her, a very large horse. Her legs collapsed and she dropped to the ground. Her entire body started jerking with agony as spasms racked her muscles. Her legs crumbled and darkness gripped her.

Michael slowed the truck when he saw a white mailbox with large black lettering and a realtor sign. He scanned the property as they passed. A white ramshackle farm house with a front porch stood about a quarter mile from the road. There was a single light that shown from the front window. A white Taurus was parked at the side of the house.

He noticed a wooded area ahead on the right. He turned onto a dirt road that led into the woods. He parked under a huge oak tree and leapt from the truck. Frankie grabbed her duffle bag, raced around the truck, and pulled on Michael's arm.

"Hold on, Michael. We can't go in yet, we have to wait for Hansen. Besides, if Beatty sees us, it will turn into a hostage situation or worse. You have to calm down. Losing control is not going to help Anne."

"Go to hell," he growled, then thought more about what she said. Shit. She was right. This was personal and he wasn't thinking like the cop he used to be. He'd seen too many raids that went to hell because a cop got emotional, jumped the gun and headed in too soon. He knew better than to let his emotions take over.

She watched him struggle for control. Relieved, she unzipped her duffle bag and pulled out her waterproof and fog-proof night-vision binoculars and handed them to him. "Come on, Boss, let's do some surveillance."

They both crouched and entered the deep of the woods. Though trying to move quietly, the dried leaves covering the ground made it difficult. Soon they saw the house in the distance. Michael aimed Frankie's binoculars toward the house. There was no movement. Beatty's car was still parked at the side of the house, and the only light glowed from the front window. He was impatient for nightfall so he could get closer. He crouched near a tree and waited.

It was his fault, Michael thought. He should have locked her up someplace safe and lost the key until the bastard was caught. He promised Anne he would protect her. Instead, he had handed her over to the killer. How could he be such an idiot? If anything happened to her, he would have to live with it. If anything happened to her, he would personally track Beatty down if it took the rest of his life.

Frankie sat on the ground cross-legged, several yards behind a tree to give Michael some space. He had calmed down somewhat, but was still riding an emotional roller coaster. She hoped that by the time they moved in, he was using his analytical cop brain.

She heard a car motor sound in the distance and looked at Michael to see if he heard it, too. He nodded. Soon she received a text from Lane Hansen ordering her to meet him back at his car.

Anne tried to move and caught herself in a groan. Her head throbbed and every muscle in her body was in revolt. She felt achy and exhausted. She tried to open her eyes, but only her right eye would cooperate. The other was swollen shut. She tried to move her arms, but couldn't. She was sitting in a hard, wooden chair with her hands bound behind her back with rope.

The room was dark and smelled of mold and mildew. There was light coming from a room to her right and she saw Beatty bending over a sink splashing water in his eyes. Next to the room was an open door to a stairwell.

She noticed the faint glow of a computer monitor on an old desk in the room, along with an ancient, dirty sofa and chair. Her purse was slung across the chair. If she could just free her hands, she could get the purse and the gun inside.

She wiggled her fingers. The rope binding her hands was not as tight as it could have been and she was thankful. Beatty must have been rushing to tie her up so he could tend to the pepper spray burning his eyes. She focused on her legs and realized she could move them freely. They were not bound.

Scrubbing a towel across his face, his eyes red and tearing, Beatty moved toward her. "You bitch!" He shouted. "You'll pay for that."

"Go to hell," she spat. Her mood was veering sharply to anger as she scratched at the knot in the rope binding her hands. He's damn lucky she grabbed the pepper spray instead of her gun.

"If I go to hell, you'll be there to greet me. You *and* your company buddies. Did you really think you'd get away with what you did to me?"

"So you got fired. Happens all the time. Deal with it." Did the sick freak think he was the only one who ever lost his job? Christ, most people in the workforce had lost at least one job in their careers. Self-obsessed bastard.

"You freaking bitch. I lost everything when I got fired. Everything!" He screamed so loud her ears rang, spittle sprayed her face and his stale breath assailed her senses.

Getting him angry wasn't helping anything. She needed to calm him down and keep him talking. It would buy her time. She prayed Michael and the police were looking for her. It was way past the time Beatty said he would return her.

"I don't understand." She focused on using her most calming voice, speaking slowly and softly. "Please tell me what happened. Tell me what you lost."

He glared at her for a moment then sat down on the dirty over-stuffed chair she'd noticed and flung her purse aside. He just sat there for what seemed like eternity, just staring and saying nothing.

The second Frankie disappeared from his sight, Michael bolted toward the house, his long legs moving faster than they had since his football days. He crouched at the edge of the front window and peered inside. No one was in sight so he moved to the front door and twisted the knob. It was locked. He pulled out a credit card and swiped.

He smiled at his good fortune and Beatty's lack of security as he pushed the door open and crept inside. He listened but heard nothing, so he moved down a hallway, his revolver pointing toward the floor. He cleared the small bedroom and closet then inched toward the next doorway. This bedroom and closet was also empty. He backed down the hall until he reached a kitchen and cleared it. There was nothing left to search but a small, glassed-in back porch and it was also empty. Where in the hell had Beatty taken Anne?

The night was now pitch black and he paused for his eyes to adjust as he walked in the backyard. He pulled out a flashlight and waved it slowly around the yard. He noted a rusty child's swing set, a wheel barrow and a clothes line. He took a couple of steps forward and swung the light. An ancient storm cellar came to view and Michael raced toward it. The storm cellar had probably protected inhabitants of the house from violent weather that raked across the flat farmland since the forties. He grasped the handle of one of the angled doors and pulled. It creaked loudly as it opened to reveal a stairwell with worn, wooden steps. A light shone through the door beyond the landing.

Michael's heart felt like it was beating out of his chest. One wrong move, and both he and Anne could die. He was an idiot for not waiting for backup, but he couldn't wait a second longer. He couldn't be that one second too late and find her dead.

Michael soundlessly took the stairs one step at a time, pausing to listen as he went. Midway, he heard voices and he strained to hear. On the landing, he pressed his body against a wall and twisted to see. Anne was in the center of the dirty room tied to a chair. Her face was bloody and a dark bruise covered her cheek. He gritted his teeth as anger shot through him. Beatty stood in front of her, screaming about something at the top of his lungs.

"When I lost my fucking job, I lost everything. I couldn't find another one in this economy, and my wife left me and took my baby with her. They're foreclosing on my house. All because of those bitches who complained. Who were they kidding? They were asking for it."

"Put your hands above your head, Beatty. It's over," Michael growled as he aimed his gun at Beatty's chest.

Beatty whirled around to face him, and then flew behind Anne's chair.

"Drop your gun or I kill her." He pulled a knife from his pocket and pressed the blade to Anne's throat.

"Take the shot, Michael. Shoot him!" Anne screamed.

He hesitated. Beatty was not very tall and Michael could barely see his chest above Anne's head. It was too dangerous to take the shot.

"This is even better than what I planned for you, bitch. You can watch me kill your boyfriend before I end your worthless life."

"Take the shot, honey. I know you can do it." Her voice was oddly calm and low.

Michael shook his head. It was still too dangerous to take.

Suddenly, she threw all of her weight to the left and the chair toppled down before Beatty could stop it. Michael aimed his gun and without hesitation fired. Blood sprayed from Beatty's chest as he fell to the floor.

The blast of the gun echoed through the woods. Frankie and Lane raced toward the house and entered through the front door. Frankie covered Lane as he cleared each room. Where had the gunshot come from? They moved to the backyard.

Michael ran to the overturned chair, untied Anne's hands and pulled her into his arms. She tightened her arms around him as if she couldn't get close enough. Relief like she'd never known flowed through her. It was over. The nightmare was over.

"Honey, let me look at you. Where are you hurt?" He looked into her face and brushed the hair from her eyes. There was blood caked around her mouth and nose. One eye was swollen completely shut.

"I'm okay, Michael. There's something I need to tell you. Something I should have told you long ago."

Holding her small flashlight above her Glock, Frankie aimed a stream of light on the storm cellar and noticed one of the doors was open. Lane was right behind her as she ran toward it. She slowed down as she reached the stairwell and took the each step one at a time as she pointed her flashlight below. The fourth or fifth step moved slightly beneath her feet, nearly throwing her off balance. She dropped down a few more steps and turned to warn Lane, but it was too late. His weight caused the step to collapse, his gun exploded, and his body slammed into Frankie, sending them both flying down the rest of the steps.

On the landing, Lane pulled himself up and whispered, "Frankie, are you all right?" She didn't move or answer. He bent down and focused his flashlight on her. She was lying on her side, still not moving. He gently pulled her onto her back. That was when he saw the blood spreading near her shoulder.

"God, no," he cried. He pressed his fingers on her wrist to feel her pulse. She was still alive but unconscious. He pulled his cell phone out of his pants pocket and called for an ambulance. He ripped off his jacket and took off his shirt, then sat on a step and scooped her onto his lap. He pressed his shirt to her shoulder to stop the blood flow and held her.

"Sweetheart, wake up. Do you hear me Frankie, wake up." He kissed the top of her head and pulled her closer.

Michael and Anne appeared in the doorway.

"What happened?"

"The step gave way, my gun went off and we fell down the rest of the stairs. She's been shot. I called for help." Lane reached for her wrist. Her pulse was slow but she was still alive. He looked at Michael. "Where's Beatty?"

"He's no longer a concern."

Frankie was having the oddest dream. She was in a dark stairway, walking down a series of steps when suddenly she tripped, but instead of falling, her body lifted into flight. Then suddenly, like a sports instant replay, she was back in the dark stairway walking down the steps, falling then flying. This continued for at least five cycles until she decided it was time to wake up. As dreams go, this one was getting boring.

She yawned and opened her eyes to look around the room. Where was she? She noticed a doorway then saw a nurse hurry past. She was in a hospital. She glanced around the room and noticed she was not alone. Lane Hansen, in a navy sweater and faded jeans, was fast asleep in a chair close to her bed. He was holding her hand. It seemed so odd to her that this huge man could hold her hand so gently as if he might hurt her, even in sleep.

Why was he in her room? And why was he holding her hand? She felt pain near her shoulder and tried to pull her other hand up to soothe it. But her hand was trapped by a sea of tubing, attached to fluid-filled bags hanging overhead.

"Frankie, are you awake?" Lane whispered. He jumped to his feet and bent over her.

She nodded and watched as genuine relief and something else crossed his face. A strange light flickered in his eyes.

"I have to get a nurse. I'll be right back."

He returned a short time later with a tall, thin nurse in tow.

"Hey, look who's awake," the nurse said with a smile.

"How long have I been here?" Frankie asked.

"You *and* your handsome man have been here for three days. See if you can talk him into going home and getting some solid sleep, will you?" She typed something on the tablet she carried, and on her way out promised to tell the doctor Frankie was awake.

Frankie was confused. Why was the nurse calling Lane Hansen *her* handsome man? And why had he slept in her room for three days?

"What happened, Lane? Why am I here?"

"Do you remember looking for Beatty? We heard a gunshot. We found a storm cellar behind his house. We thought Beatty had Anne Mason in the cellar. You went down the stairs first. When I followed you, one of the steps collapsed, my gun went off and…"

"Oh God, I remember. I had turned to tell you about the step but it was too late."

He nodded, his eyes filled with guilt.

"So that's why my shoulder hurts."

"Baby, I'm so sorry I shot you." He looked so miserable her heart squeezed.

"Lane, I don't expect you to have the superb marksmanship skills I have, but you might want to squeeze in some shooting practice," she chided him with a grin.

"Oh, yeah? When you get well, I intend to hit you up for some lessons." The tension lifted and he visibly sighed with relief.

"You mean 'hit on me'."

"Yes, that too."

"Is that a present?" she asked, pointing to a white box with a blue bow on the floor next to his chair.

He smiled and placed the box on her lap then helped her open it.

"Is that…?"

Inside wrapped in tissue was a brand-new, pale pink bullet-proof vest.

"Thanks, Lane. If I'm going to give you shooting lessons, I'm going to need this."

Michael pulled his truck up to the hospital entrance just as a nurse pushed Anne toward him in a wheelchair. He scooped her up in his arms and put her in the passenger seat.

Once in the driver seat, he turned to her, "So you're just fine, huh? You only have a broken nose, an eye that was swollen shut, scratches and cuts all over your body *and* a concussion. Only a three-day hospital stay."

"Okay, Michael. You were right to insist I come here." She rolled her eyes at him and looked away. She must look like something the cat dragged in.

"Where do you want me to take you?" He started the truck and looked at her expectantly.

"Wherever *you* are going to be," she blurted out. There it was. She'd said it.

"What?" Was she saying what he hoped she was saying?

"Remember when you told me about your favorite things and then I told you mine?"

"Yes, but what does that have to do with…?"

"I want to amend *my* favorite things list." She interrupted. "My favorite things are dancing in the dark and sharing long, hot kisses with a man that sends heat waves through my body from my head to my toes. But there is nothing to compare with making love for days with a man who has saved my life more than once. You are that man. I love you, Michael."

Michael pulled her into his arms and kissed her soundly on the lips. "Honey, you're the woman my mom always said I'd find. I've been looking for you for my whole life, and I love you so much I'm never letting you go."

"Is that a proposal?"

"Yes. Will you marry me?"

"In a heartbeat.

“What do you think about eloping? Let’s get married and honeymoon in Savannah.”

“That’s the best idea I’ve ever heard. When?”

The corner of his mouth lifted in a smile. “As soon as I can get us to the airport and get a flight.”

Dear Reader:

If you liked *Deadly Offerings*, I would appreciate it if you would help others enjoy this book, too, by recommending it to your friends, family and book clubs by writing an honest, positive review on Goodreads and your favorite retailer.

If you do write a review, please let me know by sending an email to me at alexagrace@cfl.rr.com. I'd like to add you to my e-newsletter list so that you can get updates about upcoming releases first, be eligible for prize drawings, and get free ebook alerts.

Thank you.
Alexa Grace

P.S. If you should find a mistake, please let me know. I always strive to write the best book possible and use a team of beta readers as well as an editor prior to publication. But goofs slip through. If something slipped past us, please let me know by writing to me at **alexagrace@cfl.rr.com**. Thank you.

Deadly Deception

Book Two in the Deadly Series

In *Deadly Deception*, the second book of Alexa Grace's *Deadly Series*, enter the disturbing world of illegal adoptions, baby trafficking and murder with new detective Lane Hansen and private investigator Frankie Douglas.

Lane Hansen has a problem. He needs a woman to portray his wife in an undercover operation and the only females on his team are either very pregnant or built like linebackers. Then he remembers gorgeous P.I. Frankie Douglas—a woman who could take his breath away by her beauty and take him down in 2.5 seconds. Unfortunately, she's the same woman he treated like a one night stand six months before.

Frankie Douglas has a problem. She wants to rid the world of one baby trafficking killer. The only way to do that is to partner with Lane Hanson, the man who hurt her by disappearing from her life after a night of mind-blowing sex.

They've been warned! Getting personally involved with a partner can put cases and lives at risk. Going undercover as husband and wife, Lane and Frankie struggle to keep their relationship strictly professional as their sizzling passion threatens to burn out of control.

Excerpt from

Deadly Deception

"Lane, I know you're ready to do undercover work, but with this case I need two cops who can pose as a married couple. Unfortunately, we've got three women on the team. One is built like a linebacker and the other two are pregnant."

"Sir, for this case, why don't we go outside the department? I know a Private Investigator who can handle herself on a job like this."

Newly appointed Sheriff Tim Brennan's brows drew together in a suspicious expression. "What's the PI's name?"

"Frankie Douglas. I worked with her last year on the Charles Beatty serial killer case. She's a former sharpshooter for the Army."

"Is this the same Frankie Douglas you shot?"

Lane's face flushed with the guilt he still felt about the shooting. "Yes, sir. It was an accident. We were heading down the stairs of Beatty's cellar to apprehend him when one of the steps gave way and when I fell, my gun went off and hit Frankie."

"Has Frankie Douglas done police work before?"

"I heard she's a former detective."

"I think I've heard about her. Isn't she a pretty tall blonde woman?"

"Oh, she's smokin' hot. Think Victoria Secret hot."

"Is that right? Do you have a personal thing going with Ms. Douglas?"

"No sir. Strictly professional." Of course, if he'd had a chance, he'd have made in personal in 2.5 seconds.

Brennan glared at Lane then picked up his phone and dialed a number. "Hello, Frankie, this is *Uncle* Tim. I may have a job for you. Would you please drop by my office?"

More Books by *USA TODAY* Bestselling Author

Alexa Grace

Deadly Deception (Book 2, Deadly Series)
Deadly Relations (Book 3, Deadly Series)
Deadly Holiday (Book 4, Deadly Series)
Profile of Evil (Book 1, Profile Series)
Profile of Terror (Book 2, Profile Series)
Profile of Fear (Book 3, Profile Series)

The Profile Series by Alexa Grace

Profile of Evil
Profiler Carly Stone had seen her share of evil when she worked as a special agent for the FBI. But nothing prepared her for the vicious predator who lures preteen girls to their deaths through the Internet. The analysis Carly provides to law enforcement is truly a "profile of evil".

Profile of Terror
Three chilling killers, two passionate love stories, and pulse-racing suspense with startling plot twists keep readers on the edge of their seats from page one of this heart-pounding and unforgettable romantic suspense.

Profile of Fear
A dismembered body found by a trash collector takes Detective Cameron Chase into the unspeakable world of human sexual trafficking. His county is the last place anyone would consider for sex trafficking, and that's just what the traffickers are counting on.

About The Author

USA Today **Bestselling Author Alexa Grace's** journey started in March 2011 when the Sr. Director of Training & Development position she'd held for thirteen years was eliminated. A door closed but another one opened. She finally had the time to pursue her childhood dream of writing books.

Her focus is now on writing riveting romantic suspense novels including her popular Deadly Series: *Deadly Offerings, Deadly Deception, Deadly Relations,* and *Deadly Holiday.*

Readers are describing her new Profile Series (*Profile of Evil* and *Profile of Terror*) as "edge of your seat reading from page one to the end". *Profile of Fear* is coming in 2015. Alexa's books are in ebook and print formats.

Alexa currently lives in Florida with her daughter and five Miniature Schnauzers, three of which are rescues. As a writer, she is fueled by Starbucks lattes, chocolate and communications with her street team and readers.

You can visit her website at – http://www.authoralexagrace.com

Subscribe to her newsletter at – http://eepurl.com/sJ-Df

Friend her on Facebook – AuthorAlexaGrace

Tweet her – @AlexaGrace2

Join her street team on Facebook at
https://www.facebook.com/AlexaGraceStreetTeam

CPSIA information can be obtained at www.ICGtesting.com
Printed in the USA
LVOW10s1824310515

440596LV00039B/1432/P